It was hot enough to burn rawhide, and lizards were frying on flat rocks. It was, Buchanan decided, just about two degrees fiercer than hell, and if he could keep going for another half an hour he'd allow himself a drink from his canteen.

He was in a mood for comfort, so naturally he got trouble.

He came on the troop of cavalry conducting an army prison wagon, and in the wagon he discovered his old friend, the Apache chief, Sentos, with three of his braves. It was at least 125° in the wagon. "What happened, *viejo*?" Buchanan asked Sentos.

"I was stupid," the Apache said, "I trusted a blueleg warrior, and he betrayed my flag of white. Now they wish to hang me."

Buchanan looked at the troopers and sighed. He couldn't let them hang a friend.

Fawcett Gold Medal Books
by Jonas Ward:

☐ BUCHANAN'S BIG FIGHT   14406 $1.95

☐ BUCHANAN CALLS THE SHOTS   14210 $1.95

☐ BUCHANAN'S GAMBLE   14177 $1.95

☐ BUCHANAN GETS MAD   14209 $1.95

☐ BUCHANAN'S GUN   14211 $1.95

☐ BUCHANAN'S MANHUNT   14119 $1.75

☐ BUCHANAN ON THE RUN   14208 $1.75

☐ BUCHANAN'S RANGE WAR   14357 $1.75

☐ BUCHANAN SAYS NO   14164 $1.95

☐ BUCHANAN'S SHOWDOWN   14109 $1.95

☐ BUCHANAN TAKES OVER   14063 $1.95

☐ THE NAME'S BUCHANAN   14135 $1.75

BUCHANAN'S
GUN

JONAS WARD

FAWCETT GOLD MEDAL • NEW YORK

BUCHANAN'S GUN

Published by Fawcett Gold Medal Books, CBS Educational and Professional Publishing, a division of CBS Inc.

ISBN: 0-449-14211-6

Printed in the United States of America
First Fawcett Gold Medal printing: May 1968

20 19 18 17 16 15 14 13 12 11 10

Chapter One

IT was hot enough to burn rawhide. The big horseman halted his horse and eased his frame forward, standing in the stirrups to cool his seat. He cuffed back his battered hat to drag a dusty sleeve across his forehead and twisted around to look down his back-trail.

The solitary rider was still back there, a mile or so away, coming forward patiently. Not in any particular hurry. Might be just about anybody—might have any one of a dozen reasons to be there. But it was a sudden kind of country; and Buchanan tested the ease with which the Winchester slipped in and out of the scabbard before his knee. With Apaches and scalp-hunters, Army deserters and outlaws all running on the loose, this hot Border country was a dangerous place for any man traveling alone.

It was just about two degrees hotter than hell. With a mind for the horse, Buchanan put it down the road at an easy gait. He glanced at the canteen and thought, *Maybe I'll have a drink in another half hour.*

The country stretched away flat in three directions, so flat that he judged the haze-blue ranges on the horizons to be a good forty miles away. Big enough to match Tom Buchanan—six feet plus of gentle, hard-rock muscle, with a dust-caked scab healing along his right cheek. In time it would pale into scar tissue and blend into the battle-scarred fabric of his tough, candid face. A two-hundred-pound Mexican with a chair-sized fist had laid that one open. Buchanan's slow-to-anger hands had left the Mexican giant asprawl, but the affront had been the final indignity. They could have

their pint-sized revolutions, and welcome to them. All
Buchanan wanted was peace and quiet.

He might find it up ahead there beyond the creosote
sand-wastes. It looked promising. The road lanced due
north, right up against the serrated mountain range. It
ought to be cool and green in the high country. A
crystal trickle of water, a grass meadow, some good
fishing, and an antelope haunch now and then. Put
some meat on the gaunted horse for a change. Maybe
even put some meat on Buchanan's own slab-sided
ribs. He was a big man, big as they came, but not an
ounce of it was easy flesh.

He had no grudges to settle, no appointments to
keep. Free to drift, he could discover the far side of the
hills, and as far as Buchanan was concerned, that was
what a man was made for.

An easygoing smile rested on his battered face; but
just the same, habit wouldn't let him forget that rider a
mile back. Buchanan took his time climbing into the
foothills, and it was almost an hour before he reached a
minor summit, where he could look back and command
the district behind him. When he got there, he turned
the horse around and had a look.

The rider was still on the road, turning through the
foothills on his way up. He hadn't gained any ground;
he seemed to be letting the horse choose its own pace in
the heat. Didn't seem to be much danger there.
Buchanan breathed the horse, took a sparing sip from
the canteen, and rode on.

It was a heat wave to mark down in memory. Even
here, two thousand feet above the desert floor, the
mountains wilted under the blasting sun. Buchanan
curled in and out of climbing canyons until, sometime
around noon, he heard a faint distant racket ahead of
him. It sounded like the bump and squeak of a wagon.

Before long he caught up. From a hundred yards
back, coming up around a cliff-sided bend, he spotted
the rig and recognized it: an Army prison wagon with
an escort of four troopers.

The soldiers watched him close the distance. They didn't seem particularly friendly. The rear guardsman rode twisted in his saddle with the carbine across his haunch, pointed in Buchanan's general direction. The wagon threw up a stinging pall of dust.

Buchanan had no fight with the Army and no great love for them either. He was a West Texas man, and that part of the country's experience with the Army hadn't been a happy one. Just the same, these particular dragoons hadn't done him any harm, and Buchanan was a peaceful man. He lifted the reins in both hands, showing the troopers that he wasn't wearing a belt-gun and had no intention of reaching for the rifle.

If it reassured the dragoons, they made no sign of it. One of them spoke, and the wagon stopped. The driver poked his head around the side to look back.

Buchanan let the horse carry him alongside. "Afternoon." The corporal on the wagon seat grunted. Buchanan made his voice sound amiable. "What you got inside?"

"Indians. Any business of yours?"

"I guess not. Didn't mean to spook you gents."

"Ain't nobody spooked," said the corporal. "Who are you?"

"The name's Buchanan."

"Lance Corporal Ivy. K Troop, Fifth Cavalry. Now, if that satisfies your curiosity, you can——"

He was cut off by a commotion within the closed wagon. A fist pounded on the wood; a voice called out. It made a thoughtful frown descend across Buchanan's face. The ice-blue eyes narrowed down, and he said in a more careful tone, "Just who've you got in there, Ivy?"

"Four renegade Apaches," the corporal said. He turned and yelled at one of the troopers. "Quiet them down in there, Keegan."

Keegan lifted his Springfield and banged the barrel against the wagon. "Shut up, you bastards."

There was another burst of talk inside, and

Buchanan caught one word of it—his own name. It made him swing his horse across the road. "You got Sentos in there, Corporal?"

"What's it to you?"

"The old chief used to be a friend of mine."

"You some kind of Indian lover?"

Buchanan ignored the jibe. "Mind if I have a word with him?"

"You're goddamn right I mind, pilgrim. Now, you just turn your horse around and get the hell out of here. You've caused enough of a ruction already."

One of the troopers rode forward and said mildly, "We ain't going to make that hill, Corp."

"What?"

"Look for yourself." The trooper poked his jaw toward the road ahead. It swung up a steep incline to the ridge top, stiff and precarious. The trooper said, "We'll never get this hearse up there with them four deadweight Indians inside. Maybe we ought to——"

"Shut up and let me think," Ivy said. Forgetting Buchanan momentarily, he frowned at the hill, as if that could make it go away or at least flatten out some.

Buchanan took advantage of the interruption by easing his horse back toward the tailgate. There was a small window high up in the van. *It has to be at least a hundred and twenty-five degrees in there,* Buchanan thought. When he was close, he said, "Sentos?"

A dark, square face appeared in the window, topped by a dusty stovepipe hat. "Buchanan. *Sheekasay.*"

"How're you makin' it, viejo?"

"Good and hot in here," the old Apache said.

Trooper Keegan spurred his horse forward. "That's about enough, mister. No talking to the prisoners."

Buchanan hipped around for comfort. Up front Ivy and the trooper were discussing the hill ahead. Ivy's arms rode up and down, injecting impatience into his talk. Buchanan said conversationally, "Where you taking them?"

"Fort Lowell," Keegan said.

"What for?"

"Throw them in irons, prob'ly. I wish they'd hang 'em. That ragtag bunch of old Sentos' been raising hell all over Arizona the last two years. Lucky as hell we got our hands on him and those three wildcat sons of his. And this time the Army don't intend lettin' him loose again."

The creased, weathered old face grinned at Buchanan through the little window. Buchanan said, "He always seemed like a peaceable old fellow to me."

"You sure we're talking about the same Indian?"

Corporal Ivy got down from the driver's seat and tramped back alongside the wagon. He seemed surprised to see Buchanan. "You still here?"

"Am I supposed to be somewhere?"

"You're supposed to be making dust," Ivy said. "But long as you're still here, lend us a hand. Run your rope onto that wagon tongue and help haul us up over the ridge."

Buchanan's drawl was unamused. "You telling me or asking me, Corporal?"

"Any way you like it," Ivy snapped, and turned to his men. "You boys get down and open up back here. Tie them four thievin' savages on a short picket line and unlock their leg irons. They'll have to walk up the hill under their own steam. We're going to have trouble enough draggin' this van over the top empty. And if one of these bucks lets out a sneeze, I want them dead. Got that?"

Ivy looked around. "You. Buchanan. Either pitch in or dust. Take your choice, but don't just sit there."

"What's your hurry, Ivy? Fort Lowell will still be there tomorrow." But he was agreeable by nature, so he rode ahead, hitched his line around the wagon tongue, and dallied to his horn. Engaged in this activity, he had time to puzzle over the imprisonment of old Sentos, suffering the indignity of his shackles together with his three sons. Buchanan watched the four squat Indians climb stiffly down from the wagon. Sentos stood stoically while Keegan bent cautiously to unlock his ankle cuffs. The old chief's face was so creased that he looked as if he'd slept with his cheeks pressed against a rabbit-wire screen.

Keegan roped Sentos' hands together and moved to the next Indian. Ivy kept his carbine leveled.

Buchanan spoke to the chief. "How come you got into this fix, viejo?"

"Because I am stupid," the old man grunted. "Because I trusted the word of a blueleg officer and because I expected him to honor my flag of white."

"You don't shut that mouth," Ivy grated, "I'll close it for you with the buttstrap of this here Springfield. And that goes for you too, pilgrim. Stay shet of these savages."

Keegan had the four of them roped by then, wrists bound to a common rope like four horses on a close picket line. Keegan was bending down to unshackle the youngest son—he looked about seventeen—when a new sound diverted Buchanan's attention: the clattering drum of a crowd of advancing horses.

When he looked over his shoulder, he saw a dozen riders breast the head of the slope. They stopped briefly, milling around. The leader was a barrel-chested man with iron-gray hair. Both legs were roped down around his horse, as if to hold him on.

Corporal Ivy's sharp warning reached Buchanan's ears. "Heads up. That's Mike Warrenrode and his crew."

He didn't have to say more than that. The troopers fanned out in a ragged skirmish line. Ivy said dryly, "If you value your hide, you'll step out of the line of fire, Buchanan."

Buchanan knew good advice when he heard it. He let his rope loose and gigged the horse off the road, circling down by the Indians. His practiced glance took in the nearby cover, which was plentiful; the slope was littered with big boulders.

Centering the Apaches, they waited in a loose knot

while the Warrenrode bunch cantered downslope in a determined line. Buchanan gave them each a brief scrutiny. Most of them were run-of-the-range cowboys, but two or three had the look of hardcases. Buchanan slipped his rifle out of the scabbard. If it came to a fight, he had no cause to take the Army's side, but he'd be damned if he'd get caught cold-turkey in the middle of a battle that was none of his making.

As they lunged closer he had a better look at the gray-haired leader. Mike Warrenrode, he supposed. The name didn't mean anything to him, but that wasn't surprising. Warrenrode had the face of a man to whom giving orders came naturally. Buchanan wondered again about those legs, too scrawny for the rest of Warrenrode's bulk, strapped down to the horse as if they had no strength of their own to grip the saddle.

The riders pitched to a halt in a spew of flung dust. Buchanan casually reined his horse closer to old Sentos' stovepipe hat.

Ivy took a pace forward, beside the wagon. "The major told me I might have to expect you."

Warrenrode's voice was a rolling basso profundo. "What else did he tell you?"

"Told me not to talk too much," Ivy said. "But I can talk this much. You pull any stunts, and you'll get the whole Fifth Cavalry down on you like a stampede. And ain't no big ranch nor big money can buy your way out of that."

Warrenrode lifted a burly arm, pointing at Sentos. "I want him. I've got no quarrel with the rest of you."

"Reckon I can't let you do that."

"Do I have to spell it out in blood for you?"

"I've got my duty," Ivy said stubbornly. Right then he went up a few notches in Buchanan's estimation.

But that didn't make Buchanan's place any easier to be in. His eyes made another rapid survey of the mounted men, and he singled out two of them as possible tanglers; his mind dubbed them automatically: Spoon and Knife. Spoon was round in the face and

round in the belly, while Knife was thin-bladed from
flanks to nose. But they both had smoky eyes and
too-smooth hands, and their guns hung where they
could reach them without waste motion.

Warrenrode said in a no-nonsense tone, "I want
Sentos' hide on a spit, soldier."

"Can't say I blame you," Ivy said. "But I got my
orders, and my orders say I got to get him to Fort
Lowell alive to stand trial."

"Seems to me your orders are outgunned," Warrenrode observed.

About that time Buchanan decided that since he
couldn't get out of this, the next best thing was to open
his mouth. He put his horse forward, laying his rifle
down across the pommel in a gesture of peace. "Mind
telling me what this is all about, Warrenrode?"

"If you don't know, then you've got no business
here, cowboy."

Corporal Ivy had a dry way of talking. "Warrenrode
thinks Government justice is too risky."

Warrenrode spread his hands reasonably. "You
know as well as I do what'll happen if the old bastard
goes on trial. He'll get some fast-talking lawyer from
the Indian Bureau, full of hogwash about noble savages
and busted treaties. Before you know it, they'll turn
him loose on the Reservation. And after that it'll take
him just about two whoops and a holler to bust out all
over the Territory again with a pack of young hot-
bloods. Raid every ranch south of Tucson and kill
another twenty cowhands and run off another five thousand head of prime stock just for the hell-and-be-
damned of it."

Warrenrode didn't look like the type of fellow who
ordinarily wasted his breath explaining things to drifters
and Cavalry noncoms. Right then it occurred to
Buchanan that Warrenrode was running a bluff. Warrenrode didn't have any intention of bringing the wrath
of the whole United States Army down on his gray

head. He had too much sense. You could see that much in his level, shrewd eyes.

But Spoon and Knife were a different breed from the crusty, crippled old cattleman. Those two, from the look of them, would just as soon have Ivy and the rest of them for lunch as spit. So deciding, Buchanan stirred his heels and allowed his horse to drift casually over to the side of the road, where the tilt of his rifle could lie vaguely against Spoon and Knife. Knife didn't miss that quiet maneuver; his eyes glittered, and the thin lips peeled back from his teeth in a cold, challenging grin.

Corporal Ivy had been talking. "You do your arguing with Regimental headquarters, Warrenrode. Not with me. I ain't impressed none. Like I said, I got my orders."

"You've got *my* orders now, Corporal. And I say turn them over to me before you people get yourselves hurt."

"You'll have a hard time making it stick," Buchanan put in.

"What's your piece of this?" Warrenrode demanded.

"I just hate to see the peace disturbed. It's too hot for a fight," Buchanan answered. "Besides, you don't want to get hung on account of four worthless Indians, do you?"

Old Sentos stiffened, but Buchanan shook his head at the chief. Trooper Keegan said nervously, "Corp, maybe the man's got a point. I don't aim to get killed stickin' up for these no-account redskins. Too many Indians taken shots at me for me to do them any favors."

Sentos was looking right at Buchanan, and it was plain enough what was in his mind. *You and I used to be friends, Buchanan. Will you betray me too?*

Knife's grin hardened, like a trap abruptly sprung. "Boss, we're wasting time."

"Maybe we are," Warrenrode said. "Last warning, soldier. It's up to you."

Keegan turned to Ivy. "Christ's sake, Corp, let them have them."

One of the troopers chimed in anxiously. "We can tell the major a bunch of 'Paches jumped us and run off with the prisoners."

Warrenrode said, "That's a fine idea, soldier. You just hold onto that thought while we take these redskins off your hands."

Keegan had made up his mind. "I ain't going to die today, Corp. Not on them Indians' account."

"You will on mine," Ivy answered flatly, without taking his eyes off Warrenrode. "You can start the ball whenever you want, mister. But my first bullet goes in your gut." His carbine was up, cocked and leveled.

It was in that brief, broken instant that Spoon's six-gun snaked out and roared.

The bullet hit Corporal Ivy in the chest and knocked him backward off his feet; he never fired a shot. Falling, Ivy tumbled against one of the troopers. Keegan and the others fell back, throwing themselves into the rocks; but Buchanan wasn't watching that. He was swinging his rifle around in a hurry, because Spoon's gun was coming up. It was just about lined up on him when Buchanan snapped his shot past Sentos' stovepipe hat. It knocked Spoon out of his saddle.

And then, without having to count up the odds, Buchanan knew he had to reach cover—fast.

Chapter Two

HE spilled into the rocks with a dozen bullets chewing splinters out of the granite. The four Indians, roped together, clambered into cover near him. Dragging his rifle, Buchanan squeezed himself into the boulders. He heard the clatter of horses wheeling around and had a brief sight of Warrenrode riding into the boulders hunched over—with his legs strapped down, he couldn't dismount.

Warrenrode was yelling, enraged, "You fools! I gave orders to keep those guns leathered! I'd have had him bluffed down in another minute. Good Christ, I don't intend to get hanged for this!"

Knife's abrasive voice rasped across the hot rocks. "Kind of late to turn around now, boss." His voice lifted gruffly. "Never mind the soldier boys. Get those damned Indians."

Warrenrode roared, "Trask, by God ——" But nobody was paying any attention. Iron horseshoes clattered in the rocks. Buchanan levered a shell into his rifle and caught Sentos' quiet glance; he slithered down toward the Indians.

Then a new voice came hurtling down out of the higher rocks: "My rifle's covering the bunch of you. Leave them Indians alone."

That set them back. Buchanan shot his head back, sweeping the cliffs with his gaze. Nobody was in sight. Trask—Knife—reared his horse back into the boulders. The gunfire died down. Buchanan slipped down toward Sentos, palming his sheath knife.

He reached a point ten feet above, and then all hell broke loose. Warrenrode's crew let out a ragged yell, and a fusillade opened up that sounded like Vicksburg in 1862. Bullets churned up the ground. One of Sentos' sons went down jerking, and then a second one. Sentos and the third son, tied to them, hung there helpless.

Then the newcomer, unseen on the cliff, opened up. His rifle raked the lower rocks, talking in harsh signals, driving Warrenrode's men to cover. Trask yelled orders.

Buchanan dropped down to the Indians. His knife flashed, parting the picket rope, and without talking, he rammed his shoulder into Sentos' chest, propelling the old man back into cover. The surviving son scrambled after them just in time; the newcomer's rifle had gone dry, and now Trask's guns were blasting again

Buchanan hissed, "Get the hell out of here, both of you."

But Sentos didn't stir. His bleak old eyes lay on the two dead Indians behind him. A volley of bullets screamed around in the rocks, near enough to make Buchanan blink. Sentos said hoarsely, "I must bury my sons."

"Not right now, viejo."

"Give me your knife, Buchanan. The whites must pay for this."

"Get out of here while you've got a chance," Buchanan said. "I'm telling you, viejo. You stay to bury those two, and you'll get buried with them."

Sentos' eyes shifted to his surviving son. "Cuchillo——"

Cuchillo said gently, *"Vamanos, padre."*

Buchanan didn't want to argue with the sorrow in those aged eyes, but he made himself prod Cuchillo with his rifle. "Make him listen to you. Go."

Cuchillo's young face was brown and hard. He nodded dismally, took his father's arm in a viselike grip, and spoke quickly in the Apache tongue.

Sentos protested vigorously. Buchanan, with his broad back against a boulder, slid around for a look past the rocks. It was about a dozen guns against two, which by any man's reckoning was unhealthy. His unseen partner up on the cliff was shooting sporadically at targets out of Buchanan's view. Everybody had taken to cover. It was, obviously, a mere question of time before Trask and the others would worm their way through the rocks and catch him in a cross fire. He said tautly to the Indians, "If you two light out of here, maybe I'll have a chance to talk some peace with Warrenrode. Otherwise we'll be laying the bodies out in stacks."

Sentos was stubborn by nature, but beyond that he was grieved and bitterly full of hate. You didn't talk a

man like that out of anything. It wasn't Buchanan's
words that finally decided the old Indian but something
in Buchanan's icy eyes. Sentos finally nodded his head
bleakly. The stovepipe hat wobbled. Cuchillo spoke
softly, and the two Indians faded back. With amazing
quickness they were swallowed by the rocks.

Buchanan threaded his way through the boulders,
not wanting to get caught like a sitting duck in a place
where the enemy knew him to be. The volleying had
settled down to sporadic bursts of fire.

Then he called out. "Trask! Warrenrode! Hear me?"

He got no answer; he needed none. He called, "The
Indians are long gone. Nobody left but me and the
fellow upstairs. You want to call it off, or do we have a
blood bath?"

Trask's voice shot back at him: "You think we're
going to leave you alive to talk about this, you're plum
out of your gourd, pilgrim."

But Mike Warrenrode came out of the rocks on his
horse then. "Hold your fire," he said in disgust. "Damnit, I never bargained for this. Trask, come on out
before you get somebody else killed."

"To hell with that!" Trask bellowed. His rifle
boomed defiantly.

That was when a single, cool-placed shot from the
hidden newcomer came cranging down off the cliff, hit
Warrenrode's horse, and knocked the horse down. Before the horse stopped kicking, the newcomer's voice
was rocketing down the echoing canyon.

"I've got a bead on your boss, Trask, and ain't no
way for you to get him out of there. Come out and
throw away your guns, or I'll start takin' him apart an
inch at a time."

In punctuation, his rifle cracked. It laid bare a wicked white scar along the rock not ten inches from Warrenrode's head.

Warrenrode lay helpless, tied to the downed horse.
One of his legs was under the weight of the horse, but
he didn't seem to feel any pain. He said in a tone of

powerful contempt, "How about it, Trask? You want to let this hairpin shoot me to pieces?"

There was a general shuffling, pebbles clattering, and men appearing hesitantly. Buchanan waited for all of them to come out of the rocks and walk into the open. He counted heads. Finally he stood up warily, his rifle at the ready.

Trask's baleful blade of a face watched him critically. "You ain't through with me, bucko."

"But you're through with me," Warrenrode said angrily. "All through. That's the last time you disobey my orders."

Emboldened when Buchanan didn't start shooting, a group of hands hurried to Warrenrode, cut loose his lashings, and levered the horse up to pull him out. They propped him to a sitting position against a boulder. "You hurt, boss?"

"I don't know. That leg look busted to you?"

"No, sir."

"Then, I guess I'm all right."

The four troopers, none of them having fired a shot, materialized tentatively from their hiding places. All of them looked sheepish. Buchanan walked down toward the road. On his way down he stopped to look at the two dead Indians. Sentos' sons. Then he went on down.

Keegan said, "Those two Indians hurt, Buchanan?"

"Not hurt much," Buchanan said. "Just dead."

"I didn't plan it that way," said Warrenrode, "But I won't pretend I'm sorry."

"I guess not. You'd have shot the four of them if you'd had the chance."

"I would," Warrenrode agreed. "But that amounts to exterminating vermin. I didn't bargain on the corporal and one of my own men going down. Just the same, maybe that makes the score even."

"It don't make us even for Lacy," said Trask. Lacy must have been Spoon, the round-faced one over there with Buchanan's bullet in him.

Warrenrode was squinting toward the higher cliff. "Tell your friend to show himself."

"That's up to him," Buchanan said. "You boys ready to ride out in peace?"

Warrenrode said, "You going to tell the Army what happened here? By God, Trask, I won't take the blame. I gave express orders not to fire a shot, and every man of you heard me loud and clear. Lacy opened up this beehive and he's dead. You followed his lead, Trask, and you're fired." His hooded eyes came back to Buchanan. "What about it, cowboy?"

Buchanan had to consider it. Trooper Keegan kicked dust with his bootheel and said, "I guess maybe a bunch of renegade Apaches jumped us. Killed Corp Ivy and busted the prisoners loose."

"Maybe they did," Warrenrode said, but he was still watching Buchanan.

Buchanan said judiciously, "We've got four dead here, and that's enough. I've got peace in my heart, Warrenrode, and for the sake of keeping the peace, I recollect I had dust in my eye and didn't see a thing."

"All right," Warrenrode said. He swung his finger up at Buchanan. "But like the Book says, Cowboy, 'He who is not with me is against me.' You've got a free ticket out of this country, but it's a one-way ticket. I ever see you on my land, I'll set the dogs on you. And tell that to your redskin friends."

Buchanan's only answer was a nod toward Spoon's corpse. "You can take that with you when you go."

Buchanan had kept his rifle cocked until now, when all of them were gone from the canyon. He'd watched Trask angrily bat his hat against his leg, mount up, and spur away. That parting glance of Trask's had given Buchanan an inkling he hadn't seen the last of Knife. Trask wasn't a man who'd let a grudge die easy.

He'd watched them throw Spoon face-down over a horse, watched them put Warrenrode a-saddle and ride upcanyon. And he'd watched the troopers pour Ivy and

the two dead Indians into their wagon and depart
with a squeal of axles. Ivy had been a good man, for all
his bluster.

Now that all of them had faded from earshot,
Buchanan threw back his head to survey the cliff. "You
can come on down."

"On my way," replied the hidden man.

Presently a long-legged redhead appeared in the
rocks and climbed down, grinning. His lanky frame
was cased in buckskins. One look at his bootheels was
enough to tell Buchanan that the man was down on his
luck.

The redhead swept off his hat and rubbed his face.
The startling shock of bright red hair stuck up like a
currybrush. He said, "Ten against one. You won't get
old that way, friend."

"You're the one that's been on my backtrail all
morning."

"Am I?" An innocent grin flashed across the redhead's bony face.

"I'm obliged to you," Buchanan said.

"I always hate to see that kind of odds. They call me
Johnny Reo."

Buchanan spoke his name and took the redhead's
quick, firm handshake. He said slowly, "I'm still
obliged, but I've never been a man to shoot horses."

"Saved your bacon, didn't it? Besides, I grew up in a
Mimbreño camp. Apaches figure a horse is just something to eat when you get tired riding it." He chuckled.
"I'll tell you the truth, Buchanan, I was fixin' to make
off with your horse tonight after you camped. But now
I get a closer look at him, he don't seem much better
fed than the spavined nag I was going to leave in
trade."

Reo's eyes were the color of rusty iron. He said,
"You think I look like a horse thief? Ordinarily I ain't,
but a man comes on hard times. A faro shark in
Lochiel tapped me out. You see before you a fallen

man, Buchanan. Say, ain't it just about time to eat lunch? You got any grub with you?"

While he built the fire, Buchanan considered his erstwhile savior. Johnny Reo was an irreverent young gent with a devil-may-care flash to his grin. Not the sort of fellow you'd want to trust with your best girl. Still, his laughter was contagious.

Buchanan felt the rise of the short hairs on the back of his neck. He wheeled in time to see Johnny Reo withdrawing his hand nimbly from Buchanan's saddle-bags.

Buchanan said mildly, "Nothing in there worth stealing."

"How was I to know that?"

"You might've asked."

Reo laughed, came across to the fire, and hunkered down. "Nice-looking six-gun you got packed away there. How come you don't wear it?"

"Too much weight to carry. I'm a peaceable man."

"Sure you are. You moved like a wildcat back there when the shooting started. Good reflexes. You really ought to settle down to a life of crime, Buchanan. How good are you with your fists?"

"I take a dislike to fighting," said Buchanan, without mentioning the saloons his fists had laid awaste.

While they shared Buchanan's meager victuals, Reo kept up a running fire of talk. It was happy-go-lucky and amusing, but whatever lay inside the man was effectively concealed. Reo used his talk as a smoke screen to cover his feelings; and by the time he went up into the rocks to get his horse, Buchanan knew nothing about the man that he hadn't known at first glance.

Reo brought his horse down—a spavined roan—and they mounted up. Reo said, "I'm headed for Signal town. How about you?"

"Just going up the road."

"May as well ride together, then."

Buchanan tugged his hat down. "Go ahead."

"You first," Reo said cheerfully.

Buchanan only shook his head with a tiny smile. Reo complained, "If I didn't know you better, Buchanan, I'd say a man could get shot that way."

"One of us has to take that chance."

Reo nodded briefly, grinned, and put his horse into the road.

Buchanan followed along, wiping his face. It sure was hot as hell.

Chapter Three

STEVE Quick came down out of the west pastures with an angry frown wrinkling his face. He stopped the horse just outside the Pitchfork ranch yard and lifted his canteen, downed two swallows of neat whisky, and corked the canteen. Then he rode on down past the corrals into the deserted yard.

Steve Quick had fair hair and a round boy's face that made him look a decade younger than his thirty-one years. His waxed threadbare mustache failed to give him the refined appearance it was intended to provide. He looked around the empty yard, disgusted and slit-eyed angry because old Warrenrode was out somewhere with the crew, and hadn't seen fit to cut Steve Quick in on it. It was a hell of a fine way for a man to treat his Western Division segundo and future son-in-law.

He dismounted and led his sweat-damp horse into the barn. Unsaddling, he let the horse loose into the cavvy corral without bothering to rub it down. The barn was hot and close with the stink of hay and manure. He tramped outside and stopped when he hit the open air, waiting for it to revive him. It didn't do much good; there was no wind. The sluggish heat blistered the earth.

With the shirt sweat-pasted to his back, he slammed across the yard to the long adobe ranch house and climbed onto the porch. A clay olla hung under the porch roof in a net of rope; he dipped the tin cup into the olla, filled it with water, and dumped the water over his matted hair. He put the tin cup away and shook his head like a half-drowned shaggy dog. Water splattered the door. He combed his hair back with his fingers, scraped a palm across his dripping face, exhaled a blast of air, and went inside.

The yard-thick adobe walls kept the interior a good fifteen degrees cooler than the outside. He had to stop just within the door to let his eyes accustom themselves to the dimness of the wide, low-ceilinged room; it was lit only by a half dozen tiny windows tunneled high in the walls.

Mike Warrenrode wasn't here, but his presence was in the room just the same. The massive furniture, the heavy patterned Zuñi rugs, the hairy buffalo head over the fireplace, and Warrenrode's wheelchair—all of them carried the sound and the touch and the smell of Mike Warrenrode.

Steve Quick cursed under his breath.

He lunged across the room and went down the dim hallway to Antonia's room. Without bothering to knock, he latched the door open and threw it back.

She was in her corset. Her dark eyes flashed at him. "You're always so polite, Steve."

He walked in and slammed the door behind him. A sort of smile twisted his sensual lips.

Antonia said, "You're drunk."

"Not very." He tossed his hat on the bed, and his eyes gave her a hungry appraisal. Above the black lace her brown flesh bubbled when she moved; her shoulders were smooth and dark, half hidden by the cascade of raven-black hair. She was a tall girl with big actress eyes and good bones, running just a little toward plumpness. Her waist was small, but her arms were heavy. She had phenomenal breasts.

She reached for her robe, but before she could get it off the peg, he had crossed the small room. He dragged her toward him with a grunt—and stopped short with his cheek stinging from her slap.

"Goddamnit," he roared.

She slipped away from him, twisted into the robe, and tied its belt around her waist. Quick said, "Quit looking at me like some kind of stranger."

"Sometimes I think that's what you are."

He started to give chase, but his eyes lighted on the glint of metal on the bureau. He wheeled that way.

"Race Koenig's eyeglasses. Good God. Can't you stay away from *anything* in pants?"

"He just came up here to ask where Mike went with the crew," she said.

"And he had to take off his glasses for that? What else did you give him besides a smile and a kiss?"

She said hotly, "You wouldn't believe the truth if it hit you in the face."

"Try me."

"Race didn't touch me."

He picked up the spectacles. His mouth worked. Antonia said, "He took them off to rub his eyes—he had dust in his eyes."

"Sure."

"There's no point in talking to you," she said. She sat down in front of her mirror and picked up a brush. "Just look at my hair," she muttered.

Quick moved to her and put his hands on her shoulders. "Sorry," he murmured. He bent down to kiss the back of her neck.

She slipped deftly away. "No more of that. Not until you make your promises good. I'm tired of waiting." She turned and looked up at him. "You look like your face could hold a three-day rain. It went wrong again, didn't it?"

"No."

"Then what's the matter with you?"

"Nothing important," he said.

"What a shame. And here I was hoping something dreadful had happened."

"Quit carping at me, will you?"

Her dark eyes were shrewd. "What was it this time? Did one of Madam's hookers make a sucker out of you again? Or was it Scotty's faro table?"

"Never mind," he said, snappish.

"You're a born failure, Steve."

He said, "Damn it, I can make it work without money if I have to."

"Then do it. Because I'm getting sick and tired of this hayseed desert and I'm in a mood to go East and kick up my heels."

"And leave all this behind?" he said, incredulous.

"All what?" she demanded. "I've never gotten a thing from you but promises, Steve."

He began to grin. "Not this time. I was in town this morning, had a talk with Ford, the lawyer. You know how he showed up here so mysterious-like from out West? I got the word yesterday. He's wanted in California. Something to do with a mining combine paying him off to cover up some evidence that would've set some farmer free. The farmer got hanged, and the mining combine paid Ford off, but then the grangers got proof against him, and he had to light out of California. If the California law knew where to find him, they'd come down here and extradite him before you could say Abraham Lincoln."

Yawning, Antonia patted her lips. "Is that supposed to mean something to me?"

"It ought to. Ford's the lawyer who drew up Mike Warrenrode's last will and testament."

"So?"

"Mike's will is in Ford's safe. Or at least it was until this morning."

Shrewd interest began to gleam in her eyes. "Go on, Steve."

"Mike's leaving everything to his daughter."

"Marinda?"

"Marinda. He didn't leave a penny to you, honey."

She cursed. "The old bastard."

It made him laugh out loud. "I thought that would make you feel good."

"The bastard," she said again. "I'm his daughter too, and he knows it and he knows I know it, but he's too damned proud to admit it." She banged her fist down on the commode. The brushes rattled; she said, "He'd cut me off without a penny just to keep his name out of the mud."

Quick was smiling quietly; he watched her shoulders begin to shake. Her voice came up, muffled. "I've stuck all this out for all this time—for nothing. Jesus."

"That's where you're wrong," Quick said. His smile became a grin, slashing across his face. When Antonia looked up, he drew a folded document out of his shirt. "Guess what?"

Her breath caught in her chest. Her eyes widened, glistening-damp; she finally said, "That's it? That's Mike's will?"

"The one and only copy," Quick said with satisfaction.

"Give it to me."

"When I'm ready." He put it back into his shirt and buttoned up. "When I'm ready, *querida,* and not before. You dance to my tune if you want this piece of paper, understand?"

Her face closed up and became hard. She said, "What tune, Steve?"

"Easy. You stay away from Race Koenig and anything else that wears pants. You do what I tell you to do."

"Why do you care?"

"If you're going to be my wife——"

"You don't love me. You never have."

"What?"

"You can't hide it, Steve. Not when you're making love to me. A woman can tell. Why do you care?"

"Because you and me, we're getting married." He went over to the bed to pick up his hat and stopped there to look back at her. "Do exactly what I tell you to do, querida, because I won't let anything go wrong this time. I don't aim to end up with nothing left but a fistful of busted dreams. Not this time."

She gave him a look that seemed meek, docile, agreeable. It was an act, he knew; she was a hell of an actress. She said, "How did you get the will?"

"Told the lawyer I'd let the California authorities know where to find him if he didn't come across. It was easy. We didn't have to pay him off after all."

She purred. "You're so clever, Steve." His eyes ran up and down her body; and he walked out of the bedroom, closing the door gently behind him.

He was grinning comfortably when he went into the parlor. He poured himself a drink at the sideboard and tossed his hat on the dining table. Then he got himself comfortable in the massive overstuffed chair that Warrenrode had used until the stampede had crippled him. With his dusty boots propped up on the leather ottoman, Steve Quick sat in the smell of his own sweat and brooded toward the bull buffalo head above the mantel.

There had been a time when it had been fine between him and Antonia. Their pulses had raced together, and everything had been good. But somehow it had settled quickly, like dregs. He needed her to get his hands on the ranch; and she needed him, because he hadn't been stupid enough to reveal his plan to her. Without him, she would lose out to the other daughter, Marinda—the legitimate daughter.

He'd marry her, all right, and he'd get his hands on Warrenrode's cattle empire. But he couldn't stand her anymore. Now and then he lusted for her body; the rest of the time she disgusted him. He'd have plenty of time to get rid of her after the wedding.

It was all working out. But Steve Quick couldn't help

feeling rotten. The way Warrenrode treated him, like
some kind of lackey. You'd think the old bastard was
some kind of tin god. To the manor born, for Christ's
sake. Him with his useless legs. Take him out of his
wheelchair, and he was helpless as a bogged steer. But
he treated Steve Quick like dirt.

All that would change. Maybe by marrying Antonia
he wasn't really going to become Warrenrode's son-in-
law. Antonia claimed that Warrenrode was her father,
but Warrenrode never admitted it. But if he hadn't
sired her, then why did he pay all her bills and give her
the run of the ranch? It wasn't as if he figured to bed
with her. You couldn't see the old man tossing in the
hay with Antonia, not with his legs all useless from the
Apache-started stampede that had smashed his spine.

It would work, Steve Quick decided. He lifted the
glass and drank.

The front door opened. Startled, Quick lifted his
head to look over the back of the chair. He saw Race
Koenig's tall silhouette in the doorway. Koenig was
blinking to get his eyes used to the dimness.

Quick said, "If you're looking for your spectacles,
they're in 'Tonia's room." His voice was dusty-dry.

"Knew I left them someplace around here," Koenig
said agreeably. He went back down the hall.

Quick's blood warmed up, ready to boil. He hated
Koenig's guts, ever since old Warrenrode had passed
Steve Quick over and given Koenig the job of foreman.
That kind of thing didn't rest easy with an ambitious
man, and Steve Quick was nothing if not ambitious.
But the real thing was, Koenig had got onto the inside
track with Marinda. Marinda was the logical key to
Pitchfork, but she didn't even have the time of day for
Steve Quick. Not with Koenig around.

Koenig came forward from the hall, hooking his
glasses on, one ear at a time. He said mildly, "Better
not let the old man catch you sprawled out that way,
like as if you owned the place."

Pretty soon I will, Quick thought. What he said was, "Don't let it get you all spooky, all right?"

"Suit yourself," Koenig said, unruffled.

"Just where in hell did all of them go, anyway?"

"We got word the Army'd picked up Sentos and some other Apaches. Mike went after them."

"Still out to kill himself some Indians," Quick said. He uncoiled from the chair and went to the sideboard to refill his glass with whisky.

Koenig said, "That's the old man's private stock."

"Any skin off your nose, four-eyes?"

"Don't heat up so fast, Steve."

Quick's lip curled. "You've got a bad habit, Race. You get in the way."

He went back to the chair and arranged himself insolently asprawl. "How come you didn't ride with the pack?"

"Had to stay back and mind the place. Besides, I don't cotton to killing. Indians or anybody else."

"You always was a coward," Quick said. "Afraid to die, ain't you?"

"I'm only afraid of dying badly, if it comes to that. What's in your craw today, anyway?"

That was when Marinda came into the room. She must have been in the kitchen; she was drying her hands on a towel. She was a beautiful creature, light-skinned and blonde, as fair as Antonia was dark. She only glanced at Quick; she went toward the front door and stopped to brush Koenig's lips with a kiss, then went on outside, saying something about bringing in the wash.

When she was gone, Quick smirked at Koenig. "Think you've got it all set up for you, ain't you?"

"What's that supposed to mean?"

"Slide in real easy. Marry Marinda and get the old man's inheritance."

Koenig picked up his hat and said, "You've got a mind like an angleworm, Steve—all twisted up." He went toward the door.

Just before Koenig's hand reached the latch, Marinda's piercing scream reached in from the yard.

Startled, Quick bounced out of his chair. Antonia was coming into the room, her mouth open to protest a question; and Race Koenig was yanking the door open, plunging outside.

Quick ran to the door and stopped, looking out. Before him was the tableau of the yard—the barns, bunkhouse, cook shack, corrals, windmill. Marinda was over by the washline beside the cook shack. She had her hand to her mouth; she was staring toward the horse barn. Koenig was running toward her.

Quick felt weight behind his shoulder—Antonia. She was pouring questions at him insistently, but he didn't pay any attention. He was trying to see what Marinda was staring at with such terror. Whatever it was must be out of the line of his sight, beyond the side of the barn. He went out onto the porch.

Koenig stopped in his tracks halfway across the yard and slapped his hip where his gun ordinarily would hang. He had no gun on. He stood there, raising his fists, and a gunshot boomed from the direction of the barn. Koenig staggered back, dazed. A wicked line appeared at his temple. He sagged like a drunk and fell down.

Frozen bolt-still, Steve Quick stood at the edge of the porch. Antonia came up and grasped his arm in fear. He saw Marinda walking backward, staring toward the barn as if mesmerized. She kept backing up until the cook shack wall stopped her.

That was when the two men appeared at the corner of the barn—two Apache Indians, an old one in a stovepipe hat and a young one with a Winchester rifle.

The young one turned the rifle toward Steve Quick. Quick's heart caught in his throat. He looked around wildly; he heard Antonia whimpering beside him. There was no place to take cover; the door was ten feet away, and the Indian's gun muzzle was staring down his throat. The old Indian in the tall hat shuffled across the yard toward Marinda, whose wide eyes watched helplessly.

Quick didn't move a muscle. Antonia whined; and he said out of the side of his mouth, "Will you shut up? Will you just shut up?"

The old Indian went up to Marinda and nudged her. In terror she came forward, prodded by the Indian. The old man stopped her in the middle of the yard. His stovepipe hat tipped back; he was looking up at Quick.

"Get me horses," he said.

Quick stammered. "What?"

"Horses," the old man said impatiently. "Three horses, from there." He pointed toward the corral. "Make them ready and bring them here."

Quick frowned. The old Indian's knife glittered in the afternoon sun. Marinda stood with her spine straight and her eyes closed, frightened but silent. The old Indian said, "Go now, and remember my knife."

Quick thought rashly, *Go ahead—kill her, get her out of the way for me.* But the young buck's rifle was aimed right down his throat; that was what propelled him across the yard, out of Antonia's fluttering grasp, and into the corral. He cursed and raged, trying to rope-catch three skittish horses; it seemed to take forever. Finally he had them saddled. He led them out of the corral. The young Indian took the reins away from him and waved the rifle, and Quick walked stiffly back toward the house with his back braced against the expectation of a bullet.

He reached the porch without being shot. Antonia grabbed him; her whole body was trembling without control. But the Indians seemed much more interested in the blonde Marinda.

The old man poked Marinda with the tip of his knife. She jerked back and opened her eyes. The old Indian gestured toward the horses and forced Marinda to mount up. Then he mounted a horse beside her. The young one got up on the third horse, training his rifle

all the while on Quick. On the ground, Race Koenig
was beginning to stir.

The old man said gravely, "I am Sentos. You will
tell the man who does not walk that Sentos has taken a
daughter for the two sons Sentos lost."

Without any more talk, the Indians wheeled their
horses and galloped out of the yard, leading Marinda's
horse by the reins.

Antonia whimpered and sagged against the front
wall of the house, clutching Quick's sleeve. He pried
her fingers loose and looked at her in disgust. He
looked after the Indians, watching the distance absorb
them, and finally he could see nothing of them but their
dust cloud. He turned back to Antonia. Breath was
lurching in and out of her as if she had been dragged
half drowned from the sea. He slapped her face, one
cheek and then the other, and said harshly, "Quit blub-
bering, for Christ's sake. They're gone."

"My God," she breathed; she shook her head, as if
to clear it. "My God, Steve."

"Pull yourself together," he said. "Hell, querida, that
old Indian just dumped this whole ranch into our
hands, don't you see that?"

Her eyes came around to him, baffled. "What?"

"Sure. Sentos just made off with old Mike's heir-
apparent. Don't you get it? Those Indians will pass her
around from one hut to another until they get tired of
playing with her. In a little while they'll barbecue our
darling Marinda. They did us a goddamn big favor."

He waved his hand toward the yard, where Race
Koenig was trying to get to his feet. "Better get a towel
or something and bandage him up."

Warrenrode and the crew had arrived, their horses
played out, in time to see Quick and Antonia helping
Koenig into the house. Warrenrode had exploded, and
Quick had listened with unusual patience while Warrenrode had lectured him "Why in the goddamn hell
didn't you get on a horse and go after the bastards?"

Now, with Warrenrode ensconced in his wheelchair and Koenig lying back on the divan, Quick stood by the fireplace and spoke in an even tone. "I didn't chase after them for the same reason you ain't chasing after them right now. It's useless to try to catch up to Apaches in that desert. You know it as well as I do."

"Mister, you haven't been working for me long enough to talk to me like that."

"Sorry," Quick muttered darkly.

"Be sorry somewhere else, then. I'm sick of lookin' at you."

"Sure," Quick said. He headed for the door.

Warrenrode's bull-throated voice caught him as if by the elbow and turned him around again. "No, damnit, stay here. We've got to think this damned thing out. Race, are you clearheaded enough to pitch in?"

"I reckon," Koenig said. He struggled to sit up. His head was half hidden by a thick bandage. His eyeglasses were lopsided.

Warrenrode always tended to talk in a voice other men would have reserved for use at the height of a stampede; and now, in his rage, his voice was even louder than usual. "That son of a bitch Injun didn't say anything about ransom?"

"No," Quick said.

"Are you sure?" Warrenrode insisted.

"Look, who was here—you or me?"

Distraught, Warrenrode seethed. Quick had no sympathy for his suffering. Warrenrode gave him a burning glance. "I wish I could find just one man with spine all the way up. You didn't even lift a finger, did you?"

"With a rifle aimed at my Adam's apple?"

Warrenrode muttered, "I've got to get her back." He shouted at Quick, "Bring me a drink and be quick about it. Live up to your name for once."

Quick sauntered over to the sideboard and made a drink. He could hear Warrenrode muttering to himself, "That big son of a bitch Texan. He knows that redskin. By God, he made this happen, and he can damn well make it un-happen." He lifted his voice. "Boat. Jim Boat, get in here."

Antonia drifted to the door and called Jim Boat's name. In a moment a sawed-off cowboy waddled bow-legged into the room, and Warrenrode hurled his voice at Boat. "That big Texan that let the Injuns loose. What was his name?"

"Name was Buchanan. Prob'ly still is."

"Race," Warrenrode said to Koenig, "how bad does your head hurt?"

"Not too bad."

"Then get the crew mounted. Tell them to scatter and find that bastard Buchanan."

"What for?"

"Just find him. Find the bastard and bring him to me."

Chapter Four

A cotton-ball cloud drifted lazily across the sun. Its shadow swept along the earth, flowing like lava across the dips and swells of the desert. Presently it reached the edge of a dry riverbed overhung by drought-withered trees. In their spindly shade the two men squatted by their tiny fire.

Johnny Reo said, "Don't criticize the coffee, amigo. Someday you'll be old and weak yourself."

Buchanan grunted, finished his coffee, and stood up to kick sand across the fire. Reo said, "You in some kind of hurry to go somewhere?"

"Not so you'd notice it," Buchanan drawled. "But it's sort of hot to stay put."

"Never leave till tomorrow when you can leave to-day. That it?"

Buchanan poked his big scar-dimpled jaw toward the west. "Ought to be a town out there someplace."

"All right," Reo complained, and reached for his hat. He planted it on top of his carrot hair and headed for his horse. The Mexican rowels of his spurs rattled softly.

They rode up from the riverbed onto a plain studded with a spindle tracery of ocotillo and catclaw. Reo said, "You ain't thinking of looking for a job, are you?"

"Why?"

"I'd hate to think I'd joined company with a working stiff. My policy—never do an honest day's work unless it's absolutely necessary." He grinned; the grin made a glistening slash across his face, made him look young and brashly devil-may-care.

Buchanan said, "I've never seen it chiseled on stone tablets that a man can't earn his keep."

"Don't be such a farmer," Reo said. "Work yourself to death, and then somebody's got to take up a collection to bury you. Gracias, amigo, but it ain't for me. Havin' fun, that's what we're alive for."

"Kind of hard to have fun when your belly starts growling."

"Steal a chicken, then," Reo said irreverently, and laughed at Buchanan. They topped a low rise, and from that vantage point saw a sleepy town not more than six or seven miles down the road. Heat waves shimmered and made the town look as if it were made of liquid.

Buchanan observed, "You could go straight. That ever occur to you?"

"Straight to where?"

"Someplace where you won't figure to end up gut shot out in the brush with the coyotes picking at you."

"Quit carping on it," Reo said. Buchanan shifted his glance and let it lie upon him. When Reo wasn't laughing, he had a sad face. He said defiantly, "I sleep all right."

"Sure."

"You some kind of missionary or what?"

"Just being friendly, Johnny," Buchanan said. His great good nature showed through in the mild smile with which he dismissed the budding argument. His candid eyes appraised Reo without any particular expression.

But Reo complained, "I'm the same fellow you were looking at before."

Buchanan laughed. "You've got a lot of trust, haven't you?"

"I always figured a man could only trust his dog and his enemies." Reo nodded toward the town ahead. "You reckon that town's got a bank worth bustin'?"

"I hadn't given it a lot of thought."

"That's your whole trouble, then," Reo told him. He shifted his seat on the saddle and plucked a rawhide thong from a concho. Chewing on the thong, he tipped his hat far forward across his eyes and said, "How come you came to be a friend of that old buzzard Sentos?"

"That was back in peaceable times. I used to drop by his wickiup now and then on the old Reservation before Uncle Sam moved them out on the desert."

"Drink a little illegal-brewed tulapai and swap lies, hey? But you wouldn't have become a friend of his unless you'd proved you were tough enough to keep from turning purple when they pulled a few pranks on you."

"Something like that," Buchanan said. "I was pretty good in a handkerchief fight in those days."

"Kill anybody?"

"Didn't have to," Buchanan said.

Reo grinned at him. "Reckon I can believe that, too," he observed. "For a peaceable man, you must've found yourself quite a mite of trouble here and there. And I ain't missed the fact you're a long way from home."

Buchanan said, "Maybe I have to be."

"A preacher like you? Aagh."

Buchanan dismissed it with an amiable grin. The

fact was, there was nothing back in West Texas for him
to go back to. His father had been a rancher who'd
gone broke—a drought and the bank had seen to that—
and then Buchanan'd hired on as foreman of a little
Border ranch. It got rustled clean. Chasing after the
rustlers had taken him into Mexico; one thing led to
another, and pretty soon Buchanan was hiring out his
fists and his guns. And by now what Reo said was true:
Thomas MacGrail Buchanan was a long, long way
from Alpine, West Texas.

It was a misty mother-of-pearl twilight, made that
way by steam coming up off the creek at the back of
town. The town, as ugly and lonesome as the desert
around it, was gradually melting into the earth from
which it came.

The lean, hawk-shaped man came out of the livery
stable with an angry glower. That was Trask, sizzling
because Warrenrode had fired him.

He saw two men standing in front of the cantina fifty
yards away. Ben Scarlett and Cesar Diaz. Diaz was a
scrawny little gunman; Ben Scarlett was an enormous
slab of a man, hewn from gigantic material. Trask had
seen Scarlett hurl a two-hundred-pound teamster across
the length of the barroom in the Golden Rule.

Trask went along to the cantina. In a black rage, he
hissed at the two men, "I want to talk to you."

Ben Scarlett said, "Sure, partner," and Cesar Diaz
glanced only once at Trask out of black, clever eyes.
The three of them went back under the shelter of the
porch roof and waited in silence while two men ambled
into the cantina. A freight wagon rumbled past; chains
clattered in the ox-yoke rings.

"The old man fired me," Trask said.

Scarlett said, "Hell, that's too bad."

"I aim to hit the trail," Trask said, "soon as you two
boys help me take care of some unfinished business
with a drifter."

Cesar Diaz peeled his mustache-coated lip back from his teeth. "Three of us against one drifter? You must have a powerful hate going for you."

Trask said, "Me and Lacy been saddle partners four years. Son of a bitch killed Lacy."

"What?" said Scarlett.

"*Chingado*," said Diaz.

Trask's cold glance shifted from face to face. "You boys with me?"

Ben Scarlett said, "Lacy was a pretty good man, huh?"

Diaz said, "All right. Where do we find this here drifter?"

"We'll find him," Trask said. He turned toward the door of the cantina and stopped short. Coming up the street were two riders. One of them was a rangy redhead in buckskins. The other one was a man-sized gent with truck-horse shoulders and long, whipcord legs and a battle-scarred face.

Trask said, "We just found him." With an abrupt snap of his wiry shoulders, he headed inside the cantina. "Come on. We'll work out how we'll brace him. I want the bastard's head in a basket."

Buchanan and Johnny Reo tied up in front of the Golden Rule saloon and climbed onto the porch. A cowhand went by, nodded and smiled, and when the cowhand was gone, Buchanan mused, "A friendly face, a sleepy town."

"Sodom and Begorra," Reo scoffed. They went inside.

A keg and plank bar stretched along the side wall. Several card tables were operating. The faro dealer droned, "Jack loses, five wins." The big saloon was half full.

Walking across a floor of blistered, warped planking Buchanan and Reo reached the bar. A few men gave them incurious glances. The barkeep came down the slot and inquired with his eyebrows, and Reo said, "Whiskey and two setups."

When the barkeep put a bottle in front of them, Reo looked at the label and said, "This stuff's eighteen years old, it says here. Small for its age, ain't it?"

Buchanan had a taste of it. "More like eighteen days old, if you ask me."

The barkeep gave both of them a long look and drifted away down the slot.

Reo said, "I hope one of us can pay for the cougar sweat," and cocked an eye at Buchanan.

Buchanan reached into his pocket, brought out a meager handful of coins, and counted. His eyes wandered toward the bar, where four flies were wandering around in search of crumbs from bar sandwiches. Johnny Reo's hand swept out, palm curled, and whipped across the surface of the bar. He held the fist up under his nose and slowly opened it; the four flies flew out of his hand. He grinned. "Ain't lost my speed yet," he said. It made Buchanan glance at Reo's six-gun, belted low at the hip and tied down.

In the yellow lamplight silver and gold coins fluttered across the card tables, and a haze of tobacco smoke hung under the low-raftered ceiling. Johnny Reo glanced toward the front door and stiffened slightly; he spoke without moving his lips. "Recognize the gent up front?"

Buchanan glanced that way with studied casualness. The corner of his vision picked out a small, sharp-edged Mexican bristling with guns and knife.

"No," he said.

"Name of Cesar Diaz. A little gent with a big talent with toad-stickers and six-guns. I seen him lay a few banditos out, down in Chihuahua."

"He's looking for somebody," Buchanan observed.

"Him and the big ox with him. Never saw that one before. Buchanan, I surely wish you'd see fit to wear your gun now and then."

"Now and then," Buchanan said, "I do."

"Heads up," Reo murmured. "He's comin' our way."

Buchanan, facing the bar, was lifting his glass; he did not look over his shoulder. "Which one?"

"The big ox with his nose right next to his ear. Wonder who he is?"

"Maybe Saint George," Buchanan said. "Maybe the dragon."

The big man was two inches taller than Buchanan and outweighed Buchanan by an easy fifty pounds, which made him about as big as a house. He had a rubbery leer. He aimed for a spot between Buchanan and Reo and rammed his way in with his elbow.

"Make some goddamn room," the giant growled testily.

Politely Buchanan and Reo each moved away a foot. Buchanan met Reo's amused glance. The giant glowered at Buchanan. "Ain't I seen you someplace?"

"I've never been there," Buchanan drawled. "The name's Buchanan."

"I'm Ben Scarlett," the giant said, as if it were all the introduction that was required. The best his expressionless face could do was twitch now and then, as if to drive away flies.

Reo was looking toward the front door, toward Cesar Diaz. The little Mexican was standing back against the wall with his arms folded, making an act of being uninterested.

Reo glanced across Scarlett's bulk at Buchanan. "You recognize this card game, Buchanan?"

"I've played it before," Buchanan replied.

Ben Scarlett said, "Huh? Hey, what you two doing? Ain't nobody going to rig Ben Scarlett for a cross play."

"Then back out of it," Johnny Reo said. "Stick your finger back in your nose, moose." He grinned brashly.

Scarlett's attention moved back and forth. He said uncertainly, "If you two lay a finger on me——"

"If we do," Buchanan said softly, "you won't forget

it soon. Now, I'm a peaceable man, but I can't vouch for my friend here. Maybe you ought to back away and find a place where you'll get more elbow room."

Scarlett slammed his fist down on the bar. The room rocked: two bottles fell over. Scarlett demanded, "Are you givin' me orders, pilgrim? Because I ain't——"

"You're throwing raw meat on the floor," Buchanan said flatly. "And you're getting red in the face. Now, I'm known for my gentle disposition, friend, but there are limits. If you want to play a game, then you just go right ahead and get started."

Scarlett spluttered. Johnny Reo raised his hand weakly, as if in benediction, and deliberately turned his back to Scarlett to bring himself squarely around to face Cesar Diaz.

Before Reo had completed the maneuver, Scarlett was growling inarticulately. He grabbed Buchanan by the shirtfront.

Buchanan's battle-scarred face looked almost regretful. Reflexes brought his swinging fist up before Scarlett even had a chance to firm his grip on Buchanan's shirt. The fist drilled in like a steam hammer, and there was no man alive who would be unaffected by the muscular, pile-driver force behind that blow. Ben Scarlett's breath whooshed out in a volcanic eruption. He folded over a few inches and right there began to lose interest in the front of Buchanan's shirt.

There was nobody Buchanan disliked more than a man who fought for fun. Scarlett's clumsy approach to the age-old ritual had brought Buchanan's dander up. Buchanan measured Scarlett, brushed the thick-armed guard aside, and aimed a shoulder-driven punch at Scarlett's jaw.

Scarlett's face was slick with sweat; Buchanan's blow slid off. Somebody said maliciously, "Bust him, Ben."

And Buchanan heard Johnny Reo's voice: "Pull that gun, Diaz, and I'll ram it down your teeth."

A hard sadism clamped itself down on Ben Scarlett's face. He swarmed in, right into the sledge of

Buchanan's fist. Scarlett backpedaled. The diamond-hard edges of Buchanan's great fists hooked into Scarlett's big belly; the pair of flat echoes slapped around the saloon. But Scarlett was big enough to absorb punishment, and his beady eyes narrowed down with canny earnestness. His face, as much as it was capable of expression, filled with a leer of sensual pleasure.

It was short-lived; it lasted only until Buchanan slammed him full in the face with his fist. Scarlett made a curious noise. He took a sickening jolt in the belly, jackknifed, and bent wearily right into the path of Buchanan's almost indifferently aimed left fist. It connected with the blunt point of Scarlett's jaw. He reeled and fell like a chopped tree.

Fully angry now, Buchanan braced his legs. "Get up."

Scarlett brought him into focus. "Forget it," he muttered, and fingered his jaw gingerly.

A long, hawk-bodied shape filled the front door, drawing Buchanan's attention, and Reo's. It was Trask. Trask didn't move or speak; but the distraction gave Cesar Diaz time to go for his guns.

Johnny Reo's forty-four cleared its holster in a blur. Under the low ceiling its roar was ear-splitting. It hit Diaz no more than a half-inch off dead center. Diaz slammed back against the wall and slid down, leaving a red smear on the wall above him.

Reo's gun lay trained in his fist—trained on Trask. Reo said in an easy way, "Make up your mind before you die of indecision."

Trask's eyes roamed from face to face. He settled on Buchanan and slowly raised his index finger accusingly. "You."

Ben Scarlett was getting painfully to his feet. The town marshal rushed in like a volunteer fireman, all red-faced and out of breath in his claw-hammer coat. Trask turned on the marshal with vicious sarcasm. "You're late, Yancey. The corpse beat you to it."

Yancey had a look at Cesar Diaz's body and then looked at the gun in Reo's fist. "You kill him?"

"Yeah."

"What do you call yourself?"

"Unless I want me," Reo said, "I don't call."

Trask said, "Him and that big drifter, there. Arrest them both, Yancey. The drifter picked a fight with Ben Scarlett to cover up murderin' Diaz."

Reo said, "Seems to me it was the other way around."

The marshal tramped forward like a bantam cock and threw his head back to glare balefully at Buchanan and Reo. "You two coming peacefully?"

Reo said, "We're not coming at all, Marshal."

Buchanan said, "It was a fair fight."

"Uh-huh," said Reo. "Terrible the way I lose my temper." He grinned at the marshal and waggled his gun.

Yancey was full of bluster and bravado. "This is the law talking, friend."

"Talk all you want," Reo said obligingly. "Just remember, the gun is mightier than the word."

Trask was kneeling by Diaz's corpse. When Trask got to his feet, he said to Reo, "You was just lucky."

"No. I'm good."

Ben Scarlett stumbled against the bar and croaked for whiskey. Looking at Scarlett, Reo said admiringly to Buchanan, "Amigo, when I grow up, I want to be just like you."

Looking over the two hard-bitten strangers, the marshal was hesitating. That was when Trask said angrily, "Arrest them, Yancey. The redhead murdered Diaz, and the other one helped him do it. He shot Lacy dead this morning, and Mike Warrenrode posted him out of the country."

Buchanan said, "You're forgettin' to mention that Warrenrode posted you out of the country too, Trask."

"You're a liar," Trask said.

There weren't too many things that could get

Buchanan angry, but that was one of them. He opened
his mouth to speak, but Yancey talked faster.

"Both of you shut up. Redhead, use that gun or give
it up to me. But think about what happens if you kill
yourself a law officer."

"You act like that badge is made out of six feet of
armor plate," Reo said.

"Naw. I just don't reckon you'll kill me in front of
all these witnesses. Not when you know the badge will
just get up and come after you on somebody else's
shirt."

Trask was gloating silently. Buchanan said, "You're
taking Trask's word?"

The marshall said, "I know Mike Warrenrode. I
don't know you."

Someone in the crowd spoke out. "That there's
Buchanan, Yancey. He's the man killed Mike Sandoe
in a gunfight."

Reaction hit the crowd like an abrupt intake of
breath. Yancey's eyes widened and strayed toward
Buchanan's hip. No guns there. Yancey's bravado returned.

Johnny Reo said, "It appears like if you want to find
the law around here, all you got to do is look inside
Mike Warrenrode's pocket."

Yancey flushed. "Gimme your gun and shut up."

"I'll just keep my gun for the time being," Reo said.
"But we'll mosey on over to the jail with you."

Yancey paused, looked around, and finally squared
his shoulders. "Fair enough." He lifted his voice at the
crowd. "I guess that's all, ain't it, boys? Somebody get
Diaz out of here."

Reo kept his gun. He followed Buchanan, and
Buchanan followed the marshal. The three of them
single-filed out of the saloon. When Buchanan went
past Trask, he caught the self-satisfied smirk in Trask's
eyes. Buchanan chalked that one up, too. He went
outside and followed the marshal down the street.

Inside the marshal's office Yancey shut the door and

said, "You can let me have the gun now. Ain't nobody going to potshoot you in here."

"All right," Reo said, and handed over his gun without argument. Buchanan looked at him, surprised.

Yancey went around and sat down at his desk. He took out a blank form and wetted the point of a pencil with his tongue. "How much money you two got between you?"

"Not a dime," Reo said cheerfully.

Yancey looked at Buchanan. Buchanan shrugged, turned out his pockets, and put his money on the desk.

Yancey counted it out. "Eighteen dollars. Ain't enough."

Buchanan said, "Enough for what?"

"Pay your fines."

"Fines?"

"Disturbin' the peace," Yancey said complacently. "Hell, I know it must've been a fair fight, otherwise you wouldn't of give me that gun. But if Warrenrode wants you out of the country, then that's the way it's got to be. I reckon them two crowbait nags out there belong to you, hey? Maybe I'll just confiscate 'em to take care of your fines. There ought to be enough left over to buy a couple stagecoach tickets to Tucson. Stage leaves in the morning. I'll jail you overnight just to keep you out of trouble."

Johnny Reo said, "Marshal, we got no objection to spending a night on your room and board. But you take a man's horse, and you're buying trouble."

"Is that a threat, cowboy?"

"Just advice," Reo said.

"We'll see," said Yancey. He picked up a key ring and went back into the cells. "Come on."

Locked up in the cell next to Reo's, Buchanan stood at the barred window watching the winking lamps of town. He said, "I didn't bargain on him stealing our horses."

"Neither did I. Figured he'd put us up to a free night's room and board. Otherwise I wouldn't have let him have the gun." Reo's shoulders went up and went down. "Just shows you can't trust anybody, least of all a badge toter."

Buchanan stretched. "We can worry about it in the morning. Might as well try to get some sleep."

"Amigo," said Reo, "I won't have to try." He lay back on his cot and tipped the hat forward over his face.

After a little while Buchanan lay down and stared frowning at the ceiling. He had a feeling that there was trouble in store. And Buchanan didn't look forward to that. He was, after all, a peaceable man.

Chapter Five

BUCHANAN stretched like a cat and blinked away the morning blaze of light that lanced down through the bar-latticed window. A skinny kid brought in a pair of precariously balanced breakfast trays, went without a word, and returned twenty minutes later to take the trays away. Johnny Reo pointed to his half-finished meal. "What do you call this stuff? Fried adobe?"

The skinny kid gave him a look, took the tray, and left again.

"Talkative shaver," Reo observed. "Tell me something, Buchanan."

"What's that?"

"What do you figure we ought to do about it if that bantam-cock marshal steals our horses?"

"Steal them back," Buchanan said without heat.

Reo grinned at him. "Now you sound like a sensible man. And here I had you all pegged out as a law lover."

"I tend to respect a badge," Buchanan said, "except when it's tied on a picket string that leads back to some citizen perched on a rawhide throne."

"Meaning Mike Warrenrode. You know, you and me made one mistake. We should have minded our own business and let him skewer those worthless redskins."

"Thought you said you'd been raised by Apaches."

Reo said, "That's what makes me know they're worthless," and he grinned. His red hair stuck up in a tall flaming brush.

Buchanan cocked his head toward the open door at the end of the cell corridor. "Sounds like company."

"You got good ears."

The door opened, and a tall man stooped to clear the frame. Rangy and handsome, he wore a doctor-fresh bandage over one temple, and a pair of iron-rimmed eyeglasses. He came down the hall and stopped in the hall to give Buchanan the once-over.

"How are you?" said the stranger.

"Friendly."

"I'm Race Koenig."

"That's mighty nice of you," said Buchanan.

Koenig went on to the next call. "Are you Reo? I'm Warrenrode's foreman."

Johnny Reo said coolly, "I don't know you."

"You will," Koenig said, and turned back to regard Buchanan. "The boss is disappointed in you. You're still alive."

Buchanan said, "I'm beginning to think I don't really have to get all broken up about it if your boss is disappointed. In fact, I'm starting to get a little tired of hearing about him."

Koenig said mildly, "You are allowed to breathe by the grace of Mike Warrenrode, pilgrim, and besides, a man oughtn't boil over so early in the morning. You're likely to run out of steam before sundown."

Buchanan grinned at him. He was already beginning to like the tall bespectacled cowboy.

Marshal Yancey came down the hall and said testily,

"Couple of border toughs is all they are, Race. Maybe they've got a future, but it ain't in this particular climate. I'm puttin' them on the stage."

"Not this morning, Yancey," said Koenig. "Afraid I need them for a spell."

"Huh?"

"Boss's orders. I've been looking for these two—in fact, the whole Pitchfork crew's out scouring the desert for them. I only just found out you had them in here."

Johnny Reo walked forward and put his hands on the bars. "What you want us for? A necktie party?"

"You'll find out," Koenig said, and turned to the marshal. "Let them go in my custody, Yancey. I'll take their guns with me."

"How about payin' their fines?"

"Send the bill to Pitchfork."

Yancey heated up. "Race, I ain't your lackey and I ain't Mike Warrenrode's neither."

Koenig said gently, "All right. Go ahead and put them on the stage. I'll take them off it. That make you feel happier?"

Yancey grumbled. His eyes flickered around; finally he lifted the key ring and stepped forward to open the cell doors.

Casually Race Koenig shucked out his six-gun and let it dangle in his fist, with his thumb over the hammer ready to shoot. He said, "Don't either of you do anything foolish, now."

Johnny Reo said, "If you're in the popularity contest, friend, you ain't trying very hard to win."

Buchanan stepped out of his cell, lugging his hat. He said, "I was getting tired of the food anyway."

Yancey told him, "We don't tend to encourage folks to stay that way."

"I could see that," Buchanan said amiably.

In front of Koenig's gun, they went out to the office. Koenig collected two gunbelts—Reo's and Buchanan's; it indicated to Buchanan that somebody had gone through his saddlebags. That was where he kept his belt gun.

Koenig said, "Yancey, you might go rustle up their horses."

"And I might not," Yancey said. "I told you before, I ain't———"

"You ain't about to get many votes next election if you keep bucking me," Koenig said. His eyes, wide and innocent behind the dusty glasses, lay blandly upon the marshal, whereupon Yancey clapped his hat on and stalked outside.

Koenig grinned. "He takes a little proddin' now and again."

"Like a jackass in harness," Buchanan observed without rancor.

"Something like that," Koenig agreed cheerfully. "But don't be hard on poor old Yancey. He's just what this town needs. If he was any tougher, we'd have a lot more trouble around here. Give a gent too big a dose of the law the first time, and it's just like whisky—he's likely to swear off for life. With Yancey, we don't need to worry about that."

"Must be a great comfort," Johnny Reo said.

Buchanan propped his hip against the corner of Yancey's desk. His eyes drifted around the place and for a moment he contemplated diving for the rifle rack, but before making that decision, he reckoned he ought to find out what Koenig had in mind, so he said, "What does Warrenrode want from us?"

"Just talk," Koenig said. "Ain't nobody aiming to string you up, if that's what's troubling you." His grin settled lazily, and he drifted closer to the rifle rack; he said mildly, "Don't get notions, Buchanan."

Johnny Reo said, "I rise to remark this country gets curioser and curioser."

"Don't let it fret you," Koenig said. "You might enjoy havin' a talk with the old man. Most people hate him on sight, but it takes some folks a little longer."

"Then why are you workin' for him?" Reo inquired.

"Because he's the best friend I ever had," said Koenig. "He's turned a mite testy since he got his legs stove up, but before that he was the finest man this side of San Antonio—the toughest, the biggest, and the most generous you ever met. Bunch of Sentos' Apaches run off one of our herds at roundup time a year or two back, and the old man got caught in the stampede. That's what crippled him."

"And makes him hate Sentos," Buchanan said.

"Sure. But you got to make allowances. There never was a better man to work for. You can make mistakes, long as you don't make excuses."

"Like Trask?"

"I heard about that," Koenig said. "Trask had that coming to him a long time."

He seemed about to add something, but Yancey appeared in the door, red-faced and petulant. "Your goddamn horses are waitin'," he said, and went scowling around behind the desk to sit down. "Get the hell out of here. I'm sick of lookin' at all three of you."

Koenig jiggled his six-gun. Reo looked at Buchanan, shrugged, and headed for the door. Yancey said, "By the way, Ben Scarlett's comin' down the street. Do me a favor and take him with you. I don't need his kind of trouble in town."

"He's supposed to be at work anyway," Koenig said.

Buchanan went outside with Reo and looked up-street. Ben Scarlett, big as a Clydesdale, was lumbering toward them, and Scarlett's face became hard and angry when he recognized Buchanan. Koenig stepped onto the sidewalk and said, "What fell on you?"

Scarlett poked his face toward Buchanan. "This bastard got a lucky punch." He began to square off defiantly. "This time he's gonna be picking up his teeth with two busted arms."

Buchanan said, "You know what I like about you, Scarlett?"

Flustered, confused, Scarlett took a little while to absorb it. "Huh? What?"

"Know what I like about you?" Buchanan repeated.

"No. What?"

"Nothing."

Scarlett turned a color that befitted his name. His cheeks puffed out, and he seemed to swell up. Koenig stepped between them casually, and said: "Go get your horse and catch up to us, Ben. We're headed for Pitchfork. You can settle your grudges some other time."

Scarlett's hound face turned sluggishly toward Koenig. "Yuh," he muttered. "Sure, Race." He shouldered past and went down the street.

Johnny Reo said, "He's a buzzard, ain't he?"

"Maybe," said Koenig. "But don't forget, a buzzard can spot a helpless field mouse from five thousand feet up."

Marshal Yancey appeared in the door. "You all still here?"

"Just on our way," Koenig said.

The marshal squared his narrow shoulders. "Tell your boss something for me, Race. Tell him I'm sick and tired of being treated like one of his hired hands."

"I'll tell him," Koenig said. "But just think about the fix you'd be in if Mike Warrenrode pulled out his support. You've got a lot of enemies, Yancey."

Koenig stepped down into the street and said, "I leave you with that thought, Yancey. It ought to keep you from getting bored." He gestured with his gun toward the waiting horses. "Put it in the saddle, gents."

The wagon road took them across rolling desert hills. Two miles out of town, Ben Scarlett caught up, riding a horse as big as any Buchanan had ever seen. Scarlett still thought it was a lucky punch that had floored him last night. Koenig, whose orders Scarlett seemed to respect grudgingly, had to restrain Scarlett from jumping all over Buchanan.

Even Buchanan's extraordinary equanimity had its limits. By the time they raised sight of the Pitchfork buildings, he had had his fill of Scarlett's epithets. He

was ready to meet Scarlett more than halfway. They
rode down a gentle pitch into the yard. Buchanan's
practiced scrutiny took in the buildings and corrals
briefly, and he conceded silently that the ranch was a
model of perfection, expertly managed and well kept.
He wondered how much of that was due to Race
Koenig's talent. Koenig impressed him as an earnest,
skillful cattleman, good-natured but tough.

A full-breasted, dark-haired girl stood in the ranch
house door, shading her eyes with her palm.
Buchanan's interest was drawn wholeheartedly that way
when they halted their horses in the yard. Buchanan
began to grin, which was when, with his fragile self-
control snapping like a brittle twig, Ben Scarlett
launched himself from the saddle and butted Buchanan
right out of the saddle.

The two big men landed in a heap amid milling
horsehoofs. Buchanan struck the earth on shoulder and
flank and felt the slivers of bruising pain. With dust in
his eyes, he got untangled and circled away, getting his
feet under him. He wiped his face and braced himself,
and heard Scarlett mutter, "I am going to break a few
of the bones you need the most."

Buchanan brought up his guard—and a wheeling,
riderless horse, his own or Scarlett's, spun against him,
knocking him asprawl. He hit the dirt with his face and
heard Scarlett's grunt of pleasure. Scarlett landed on
top of him like two tons of horseshoes, hooking his
thick arm around Buchanan's windpipe while he kept
both knees planted in Buchanan's back.

Men swarmed into the yard from the bunkhouse and
barns to watch. Koenig's angry voice was rising and
falling, but the milling horses kept cutting him off.
Scarlett's hot, acrid breath whooshed against the back of
Buchanan's neck. Locked in Scarlett's grotesque hold,
Buchanan felt himself being bent backward unnaturally, with the breath cut off at his Adam's apple. The
gathering crowd murmured, and the murmur grew into
a growl and became a red, flooding roar in Buchanan's

ears. A pulse throbbed in his head; a blood-thick haze climbed up like a curtain over his eyes. Purple-faced, far past the point where a lesser man's neck would have broken, Buchanan finally found a subtle point of balance and used it as a lever; the crooked point of his elbow smashed brutally backward into Scarlett's ribs.

Scarlett's grip slackened ever so slightly—but it was enough for Buchanan to wedge his upthrust shoulder inside the curve of Scarlett's arm. With that advantage, Buchanan humped his back, heaved his shoulders upward, and let himself fall to one side, pinning Scarlett's arm under the weight of his shoulder. Elbow driving like a piston, he finally broke loose and rolled away, heedless of the dancing hoofs around. As his vision cleared he had a clear instant's view of one horse's rolling eyes.

He heard the dark-haired girl shrieking, "Kill him! Kill him!" It wasn't clear which one of them she had in mind. He had time to think, *Bloodthirsty wench*, and then he was dodging out from under the belly of a rearing horse, getting his feet under him, wheeling, trying to find Scarlett in the dusty confusion. Koenig tramped forward on foot with his six-gun out, but then Buchanan found Scarlett. He brushed past Koenig's gun, too angry to think about it, and roared into Scarlett like a tornado.

"Put him on the ground," the girl shrieked. "Hard!"

He waded in, assuming she was rooting for him but not really caring. He caught Scarlett in the soft belly and buried his fist up to the wrist. He pulled it out and clubbed Scarlett's nose with it. He used it to drill holes in Scarlett. It had all of Buchanan's formidable weight and all the incredible muscle power of his right shoulder behind it. It plunged in a blur of motion against Scarlett's belly, Scarlett's neck, Scarlett's hapless face. It made sickening sounds that clapped echoing around the yard.

The open-mouthed gawking cowboys watched mutely while Ben Scarlett's knees went rubbery. Scarlett made a dainty pirouette, turning half around as he sank, then collapsed senseless.

Buchanan looked around, his anger beginning to cool down, and went hunting for his hat.

The dark-haired girl pushed through the crowd and grinned at him. Buchanan crushed his hat down on his head. He turned toward the girl—and saw Scarlett, moving sluggishly, dragging out his holster gun.

Koenig's long leg thrashed out. His boot cracked against Scarlett's wrist. The gun dropped away.

Koenig said, "Don't lose your head, Ben. Fun's fun."

Johnny Reo said, "He ain't losing his head. He's losing his nerve."

Dust settled. The girl came up to Buchanan with a smile that was as good as a kiss. "What's your name?"

"Buchanan."

"I seem to remember you," she said, "from one of my better dreams." She attached herself to his arm like a hungry leech.

Steve Quick took three steps forward and grabbed the girl. "Jesus. You got no sense at all?"

Koenig said, "Antonia, this ain't no place for you. Get her back in the house, Steve."

Quick said, "Damn right." He jerked on the girl's arm.

Buchanan said gently, "Ease off," and gave Steve Quick a gentle look, which persuaded Quick, after a look at the dazed Scarlett, to drop his hand and back away.

Antonia smiled up at Buchanan. "I think I could learn to like you."

Johnny Reo said, "Bet your bottom."

The girl hip-swayed away. Race Koenig said, "Where's the boss?"

Steve Quick said, "In the house."

Koenig said, "All right, everybody get back to work. You two come inside with me."

Johnny Reo fell into step beside Buchanan. He said,

"You can dream up some pretty weird things in this country."

"You can meet some too," said Buchanan.

Chapter Six

MIKE Warrenrode spoke from his wheelchair "Take the gentleman's hat, Race."

Koenig looked at Johnny Reo, who made a face and took off his hat.

Warrenrode said, "I don't want to look up at you people. Sit down."

Buchanan drawled softly, "I reckon I'll just keep my feet."

Warrenrode's lips pinched in. Seated beneath the Seth Thomas clock, he said, "All right, Race. Leave us alone."

"You sure?"

"Get out."

Koenig, with a worried look, glanced at Buchanan and Reo before he went outside and pulled the door shut behind him.

Warrenrode said, "Whisky in the sideboard. Help yourselves."

Reo went that way. Warrenrode addressed himself to Buchanan. "I hear Ben Scarlett will never be quite the same again. You're quite a stemwinder, aren't you? What was your name again?"

Warrenrode ashed his cigar in the tin ashtray at his elbow. His skinny legs protruded beneath a blanket tossed over his knees; but from the waist up he was a formidable block of a man, bushy-haired and fierce of countenance. Johnny Reo handed a drink to Buchanan and then walked to the easy chair and sat down, poking his boots out.

Warrenrode snapped, "See your spurs don't rip that rug."

"And if they do?" Reo said in a voice dry as the desert wind.

Warrenrode grimaced. "You two couldn't get ten feet from this house without safe conduct from me. Let's not waste time exchanging threats, gents."

Buchanan said, "If you're coming to a point, let's hear it."

Warrenrode shook his head; a vast weariness seemed to overcome him. "Some days I wonder if I'll make it through to sundown."

Reo said, "Careful you don't sorrow yourself into an early grave."

"If a man's pitiable, then you can't criticize him for self-pity," Warrenrode said. "That Indian you broke loose yesterday—old Sentos—he came by this place yesterday to steal some horses."

Buchanan watched him guardedly. Johnny Reo said, "Look, friend, I don't like bein' put on the carpet, and I don't aim to take the blame for you losin' a horse or two."

The old man's eyes, full of misery, came up and locked on Buchanan's. "Horses wasn't all they took. He packed my daughter. Marinda, away with him."

Buchanan absorbed it without a break in expression; but he said, "Looks like you've got a burden."

"I do," Warrenrode said. "I love that girl, mister. I want her back."

"Good luck," Reo muttered. "I reckon you know what they do to white squaws."

"I know this much," Warrenrode said. "They don't kill them. Not right away. She's still alive, somewhere back in the mountains in that old bastard's camp. I will not think about what they're doing to her." He stirred in his wheelchair; he said, "I'm a gambler. I hate your guts, Buchanan, but you look to me like a good risk, and I know you're a redskin-loving friend of the old son of a bitch. And you, redhead, I make it you were the gent up in the rocks with the rifle."

"Could be," Reo said.

"Good shooting. Damn good."

Reo said, "Get at it, then."

"I will. If a man's sick, he calls a doctor. I'm calling on you two. I want my daughter back alive."

Buchanan said, "I'm a little fuzzy this morning. I thought I heard you say you want us to go after your daughter."

"How about it, Buchanan?"

"I'd sooner herd sheep," Buchanan said. "I've trapped beavers and a few rabbits in my time, but I leave Indian-trapping to the missionary priests."

"You don't get me," Warrenrode said. "It's gone beyond revenge. I can't send an armed force after those Indians. It would just get Marinda killed. There'll be time afterwards for me to devote the rest of my life to getting my hands on the red bastard and tearing him apart one bullet at a time. Right now that's beside the point."

Reo said, "Then, what *is* the point?"

"Get her back," Warrenrode said.

Buchanan said, "Two white men riding into Sentos' stronghold up in those mountains would have about as much effect as a handful of snow on a forest fire."

"Two ordinary men," Warrenrode said. "But you just might be able to do it. Sentos' friendship for you may be the one thing that can save my daughter. He owes you his life, for yesterday. Use that against him. Persuade him. Hell, I don't care what you decide to do. Do it—ask me how later."

Buchanan sipped his drink, walked to one of the high windows, and peered out through the thick wall at the brilliant sky. His face was narrowed down into a scowl.

Mike Warrenrode leaned forward, elbows on the

arms of his wheelchair. "I'm sure you'll decide to do it."

"Don't be sure," Buchanan said. "The odds are bad."

Warrenrode said, "If I seem abrupt and rude, it's because I am. But you ought to know this. If you two want to stay alive in this country, you're going to have to do it for me."

Buchanan wheeled slowly on his heels and shook his head. "Not that way, old man. Nobody crowds me into anything."

"I will if I have to. I'll be honest with you. I've got no choice. You ride for me or you die."

Johnny Reo said, "I always tend to suspect a man who starts out by saying, 'I'll be honest with you.' "

Buchanan said, "Anything can happen up in those mountains. There are a lot of Apaches up there. My friendship with Sentos won't save our hides if other Indians spot us first."

Johnny Reo said dryly, "You want to try a crystal ball or tea leaves?"

Buchanan said, "Let's use cards. Let's put them face up on the table. The chances of getting the girl out of there are no better than a hundred to one."

"Doesn't matter," Warrenrode said. "It's a chance I've got to take. If it's a long shot and if it's the only shot you've got, you shoot it. Buchanan, you cut those Indians loose. When you did that, you made yourself responsible for what they did afterwards. But if you don't want to look at it that way, there are two other things you've got to think about. One is that if I don't get your word on this, you'll never leave this house alive. And the other is that I'm willing to pay for the risks you take. Two thousand dollars to each of you if you get my daughter back safely."

"I never figured to be the richest man in the graveyard," Reo said. He finished his drink, walked over to the sideboard to refill it, and abruptly wheeled. "Five thousand."

"What?"

"I want five thousand dollars from you, old man, or it's no go."

"You're out of your mind."

"And you're out on a limb," Reo replied.

Warrenrode's attention moved to Buchanan. "How about it?"

"I'll think it over."

"You already have."

Buchanan shrugged. "You kind of sneaked that one up on me, about responsibility for the kidnaping. I reckon part of it's my own fault and I don't see any way to get around that."

Reo said coolly, "Half now. Twenty-five hundred in gold."

Warrenrode said, "I don't think so."

"I do," Reo replied. He grinned at Buchanan. "What you don't ask for, amigo, you don't get."

Warrenrode said, "Where are you going to spend it? In an Indian camp?"

Reo countered, "How do we know you'll pay off if we bring the girl back?"

"All right," Warrenrode sighed. "Suit yourself. But woe betide you if you try running out with the money. My crew will track you to China if they have to. Whoever eats my bread is obliged to sing my songs, mister, and don't you forget that for a second."

Reo downed his second drink and shook his head. "Money or no, we're just liable to spend the rest of our lives all shot to pieces."

Buchanan nodded. At the window he was looking out across the desert; and he was thinking, *The only shade a man can find out there is his own shadow.*

Chapter Seven

STEVE Quick was lounging beside the house when Buchanan and Reo came out. Quick looked as though he hadn't a care in the world—but he was standing right by the open parlor window. He pushed away from the wall, walked out into the yard, and intercepted Buchanan and Reo. Reo was carrying a rawhide poke, heavy enough to be full of gold.

Quick sized them both up and said, "If you gents want a decent funeral, you'd better leave a few double eagles for us to hand over to the undertaker."

Reo said, "Who are you, mister?"

"Name of Steve Quick. Western Division ramrod here, so watch your language."

"We're impressed," Reo said. "You want anything?"

"No," Quick said. "Just wanted a close look to see what a couple of corpses look like when they're walking around."

Reo glanced at Buchanan. "I think this gentleman's beggin' for some tutoring."

"He'll keep," Buchanan drawled. "Let's get going." But before Buchanan turned away, Steve Quick felt the hard force of the big Texan's eyes.

Quick watched the two men walk toward the stable. A cowboy, who had been summoned to the ranch house, trotted out of the house and ran past Buchanan into the stable. Reo and Buchanan stood by the stable door, Reo turning up a cigarette and cupping his hands to light it; the two of them looked hard-bitten and tough in the glare of sunlight. The house door swung open, and Mike Warrenrode rolled his wheelchair into the opening; he sat there and watched while the cowboy

60

brought two big fresh horses out of the stable, rigged with Buchanan's saddle and Reo's saddle. Race Koenig approached the stable and said something that made Reo's face flash around. Reo said something, gesturing angrily. Buchanan murmured a few words. Koenig stepped back, smiling without mirth, and the two mounted up. Buchanan settled his seat and accepted the belted six-gun and rifle that Race Koenig handed up to him. Koenig gave Reo his guns, and when Reo buckled on his revolver, his red-topped face came around and aimed speculatively at Mike Warrenrode.

Quick tipped his shoulder back against the wall and watched while Buchanan checked his weapons and put them away; while Reo tugged his hat down and lifted his reins to go; while a new shape—Antonia's—came hip-swinging into sight and swayed toward Buchanan. Quick stiffened in anger but kept his place and only simmered while Antonia spoke to Buchanan. Buchanan's face was hidden by his hatbrim as he looked down from the saddle and Quick could not make out the nature of the big Texan's reply; but whatever it was, it evidently rebuffed Antonia, who stepped back archly while Buchanan gigged his horse out of the yard. Reo spurred along.

Quick stood silent and motionless, his eyes narrowed down, until the two riders dissolved into the shimmering hills, their passage marked by a plume of dust.

Antonia came toward the house, and Quick moved out to intercept her. "Walk off a little piece here with me," he said.

She went with him, around past the end of the house. "What are you smiling about?" she asked.

"Am I smiling?" He touched her arm. "That's when you've got to watch me closest."

"My, what startling news that is," she said, and gave him a mock smile.

He said, "That was a waste of time, making eyes at the one that whipped Scarlett."

"I didn't think it was. I think I could learn to like him."

Quick said, "You won't have time. I aim to kill him."

His eyes widened. "You really are jealous, aren't you?"

He began to deny it; then thought better of it; he only smiled at her. She said, "I knew one day I'd find out if you really still loved me."

"Sure I do," he said.

"I'm glad, Steve. Because I'm getting scared. Sometimes I can't stand being alone at night."

"Scared of what? Everything's going to be just fine and dandy. You just do what I tell you to do when the time comes." He pulled her toward him and dropped his mouth on hers in a hard, cruel kiss. She melted against him. He was conscious mainly of the dust grit on his skin and the unpleasantness of the heat. After a moment he drew away and said, "I've got some business to take care of. You stick close to the house and be nice to the old man."

"The old son of a bitch," she replied. "You think I'm going to forget how he cut me out of his will?"

"You might as well. Because I've got the will now, and if you play your cards right, nobody will ever see it but you and me. You're set to inherit this whole shebang, querida."

"Unless those two get Marinda back."

Quick said, "I kind of get a feeling they won't." With an enigmatic smile he left her and walked toward the stable.

After a ten-minute prowl around the ranch buildings Quick finally turned up Ben Scarlett. The giant was sitting on the edge of a cot in the bunkhouse, nursing his hurts. Quick said conversationally, "This hot sun makes a fella impatient, don't it, Ben?"

Scarlett growled something inarticulate and pressed a damp towel to his face. Quick sat down gently on the bunk across the aisle and tipped back his hat. He rolled a cigarette and offered it to Scarlett. The big man's bruised face shifted toward the cigarette, then toward Quick's face. Scarlett accepted the cigarette and watched him with suspicion.

Quick twisted the points of his scraggly mustache. He said in a very casual way, "You know, if I were you, I wouldn't take kindly to being made a fool of."

"Ain't nobody made a fool of Ben Scarlett. He hit me when I wasn't lookin'. Next time I'll tear his arms off and use them to beat his head in."

"I reckon the Indians will take care of that," Quick said. "You don't need to worry none about Buchanan anymore. But that ain't what I meant."

"Then what did you mean?"

"You ever stop to think why Buchanan made a point of picking those fights with you?" Quick knew full well that Scarlett had picked the fights, but he also knew the way Scarlett's slow mind worked.

It didn't take Scarlett long to come around. Scarlett said, "No. Why?"

"You never saw Buchanan before, did you?"

"Never did."

"Then he couldn't have had any grudge against you."

"Naw."

"Then somebody must have put him up to it, right?"

"I dunno," Scarlett said; his slow brain was grappling with it all. "I mean, Trask told me to——"

"Forget Trask. Trask's a friend of yours. He wouldn't want anybody to beat up on you. No, it's clear as crystal, Ben. Somebody paid Buchanan to trick you with that dirty fighting of his. Somebody hired him to work you over—he's a professional, no question of it."

"But who?"

"Somebody with a grudge against you, Ben."

"Could be anybody," Scarlett allowed. "I've beat up on half the folks in the county one time or another."

Steve Quick said in a soft, suggestive tone, "You remember when you used to be segundo on this ranch, Ben?"

"Hell, yes. I worked damn hard for that job, too. Then the old bastard———"

"Mike Warrenrode. He caught you busting a wild bronc with a beer bottle instead of gentling it the soft way. He took your job away and made you a common cowhand again. I don't think that was fair, do you?"

"Goddamn right I don't," said Scarlett.

Quick murmured, "You've got a lot of good friends on this crew, Ben. Men who respect you. That's why Warrenrode never fired you. He was afraid the rest of the crew would quit."

"Is that so?" Scarlett said, pleased.

It was not so, not for a minute, but as far as Steve Quick was concerned, the only time it was worthwhile telling the truth was when a lie wouldn't do as much good. He knew that Ben Scarlett, a man of methodical brutality, had nursed a grudge against Mike Warrenrode ever since Warrenrode had busted him back to the ranks. The only reason Scarlett hadn't beaten Warrenrode to a pulp was that Warrenrode was a cripple, and even Scarlett's sense of values recognized that beating up on cripples was not a useful thing to do. It had been years since Warrenrode had demoted Scarlett, but Scarlett hadn't forgotten, and neither had Steve Quick. Quick was a man who stored little facts like that in his head until they became weapons in his arsenal.

"No," Quick purred, "Warrenrode never fired you because he couldn't afford to. But he's always been afraid of you, always wanted to get rid of you. That's why he hired Buchanan—to beat you to death or scare you out of the country. But they didn't figure on you being as strong as you are. Buchanan just wasn't man enough to tear you apart, was he? You're still rarin' to go."

"You bet your boots I am," Scarlett said. "Next time I lay my hands on that fancy Texan, I'll—"

"I told you, Ben," Quick said patiently, "he's on his way into Apache country, and the chances are he'll never come back."

"But if them Injuns leave anything of him for me, I aim to——"

"Forget Buchanan," Quick said. "He was only a tool anyway. Mike Warrenrode's tool. He's the one you got to be thinking about. It was Warrenrode set it all up."

"Yeah," Scarlett said slowly, "that's so, ain't it?"

"Sure it is."

"I got to look out he don't do it again," Ben Scarlett said. A gleam came into his eyes. "Unless I look out, he'll hire somebody else. Maybe have me knifed or bullet-shot next time."

"Goddamn right," Quick agreed. "You've got to be on your toes, Ben."

Scarlett slammed his enormous fist into the slab of his left palm. "Steve, I'm in a tough place. I can't go beat up Mike Warrenrode. He's a cripple. The hands would string me up."

"Warrenrode knows that. That's why he's so bold about having you picked on. He wants to drive you out of the country, Ben, but he doesn't want anybody to know it's him that's behind it. You aim to let him get away with it?"

Scarlett shook his head in agony. "I don't rightly see how I can stop it."

In a very quiet way, Quick said, "It only takes one bullet, Ben."

Scarlett's eyes came up. They looked like two holes burned in a blanket. Quick put his hands on his knees, preparatory to rising; he said, "It's you or him, Ben. Think about that."

"You want me to shoot Mike Warrenrode?" Scarlett said, confused.

"I don't want anything, Ben. I just work here. I ain't got no axe to grind. But I'm a friend of yours, you know that, and I just reckoned you ought to know what Mike Warrenrode was doing against you, behind your back."

Quick got to his feet, acting like a very unconcerned man, and made his way without hurry to the door. Scarlett's voice reached him there and stopped him.

"Steve?"

"Yeah?"

"I'm much obliged to you for tellin' me."

"Ain't nothin' between friends, Ben."

"Steve?"

"What?"

"I aim to get back at him for sneakin' around at me that way. Ain't no man alive can get away with makin' a fool out of Ben Scarlett. Not and live to tell about it. So I'm gonna——"

"I don't want to hear about it, Ben," Quick said gently. "What I don't know, I can't repeat afterwards. Know what I mean?"

A slow grin spread across Scarlett's black-and-blue face. "Yeah, sure, Steve. Anybody asks you, you don't know nothin' at all."

"That's right, Ben."

"Steve?"

"What?"

"Thanks, Steve. You're about the only real friend I got."

"You've got plenty of friends, Ben. The whole crew's on your side." Quick smiled a friendly smile and went outside. As soon as he hit the sunlight, the smile fell away from his face. The door banged behind him. He went plowing through the yard in a dry thickness of heat and dust.

Race Koenig was just coming out of the barn. "I've been looking for you. Better get your crew back in those brakes up west of Council Tanks and start combing out cows. We've got work to do around here."

"Later," Quick said. "I got business to tend to."

"Whose business?"

"Pitchfork Ranch business," Quick snapped. "Send some other hired hand out to the brakes."

Beneath his white bandage, Koenig's weather-beaten face reddened. He took off his glasses and squinted. "Steve, I've had just about enough from you. When you get an order, you jump to it. I'm the straw boss around here."

Quick started to retort, then closed his mouth. There was no point in showing his hand too early; soon enough Koenig would find out what side his future was buttered on. So Quick just nodded and said, "All right, all right. Don't get yourself all lathered up."

Without waiting further conversation, Quick tramped into the stable barn. With an expression of decision, he reached down a coiled rope and stalked back through the aisle into the horse corral.

A dozen animals milled restively around. Quick snaked out a loop and walked forward. His dun shifted around in the midst of the knot of horses. Cursing, Quick slapped one of them on the flank with the loop end of his rope. The horses started to wheel spiritedly around the corral, throwing up stifling clouds of dust and straw and raising the smell of manure. It made Quick sneeze. He dodged back and forth, pursuing the dun into a corner. He laid his loop back, ready to throw, and then the dun dodged past him. Quick mouthed a progression of oaths, becoming furious. He saw Koenig standing outside the corral, watching amusedly, and he had an impulse to drag out his gun and shoot Koenig in his tracks, but he didn't; things were working out too smoothly just now, and he didn't want to take any chances. Personal grudges could wait. Right now there was business to take care of. Only it had to be done quickly, and the damned horse wasn't cooperating. He cursed and plunged forward, wheeling the lasso slowly overhead, waiting for a clear chance at the dun.

Finally, half choked by dust, he got his loop over the dun's head, led it into the stable and tied it up. When he couldn't find his own bridle, he swore, took down another bridle, and found that it was not adjusted to the size of the dun's head. He ripped a fingernail adjusting the buckles.

The dun tried to chop his finger off when he pried the bit between its teeth. Spooky from Quick's mood, the horse shook off the saddle blanket. Quick pinched his lips together, put the blanket back on, heaved up his saddle, and planted his boot against the dun's belly to haul up the cinch.

He led the dun out into the yard, gathered the reins and mounted up.

The horse exploded. It swapped ends, snapping Quick's neck cruelly, and reared up, trying to pitch him off. Quick locked his grip on the horn, sank spurs deep into the dun's ribs, lashed it with his hat, and grimly cursed the beast.

The horse lined out in an angry gallop. At least, he thought, it was headed in the right direction—the road to Signal town.

He tied up outside the cantina, leaving the horse sweat-lathered and heaving. The noonday heat slammed down viciously on the weathered town.

Nobody was inside except the bartender. Quick slapped a coin down on the bar. "Seen Trask?"

"I don't think so, señor."

"This half eagle's yours if you find him for me. Tell him I'm waiting here for him. And make it quick. I'll mind the store."

"*Si*," the barkeep said. He snatched up the coin, pocketed it, and went out.

Quick went around behind the bar and helped himself to a glass of forty-rod whisky.

The flush in his cheeks was not altogether from the heat. Excitement stirred him; he could not stand still. He drifted aimlessly around the empty saloon, kicking chairs, sipping from his drink, pulling out his pocket timepiece and opening the snap lid and looking at it

and closing it and putting it away. If anyone had asked
him the time, he would not have been able to answer
without looking at his watch again.

Finally Trask came in, stopped, and watched Quick.
Trask's attention was like the blade of a knife, motionless but ready to cut. The bartender came in and went
around the bar. Trask walked back to the end of the
room and waited for Quick to come over, and said,
"Want something?"

"You did a bad job on Buchanan last night."

"Who told you about that?"

"Ben Scarlett."

"Someday," Trask said, "somebody's going to shut
that big stupid mouth for good."

"Don't fret yourself about him," Quick said. "I came
to town to offer you another chance at Buchanan and
his partner."

"Reo?"

"You know him?"

"Heard about him. He'd set fire to his own mother if
he could get a good price for the ashes."

"That's interesting to know," said Quick, and he filed
it away in the recesses of his mind. "Look, you want
another crack at Buchanan?"

"He killed Lacy and he killed Cesar Diaz, or anyway
Reo did. Sure I want another crack at him. Son of a
bitch cost me a good job at gun wages. Where do I find
him?"

"The two of them headed southwest from Pitchfork."

"Southwest? Toward Indian country?"

"They're headed for Sentos' camp."

"I'll be," said Trask.

"Uh-huh," Quick said. "You'll need a couple gunnies to go along with you. Buchanan and Reo's too
much for you to take on by yourself."

Trask said dryly, "I gather you ain't cuttin' yourself
in."

"I've got some other fish to fry. But there's two

hundred dollars in it for you. Split it any way you like with the boys you hire."

"What's your piece of this?" Trask said.

"Strictly business. I've got my reasons for not wanting Buchanan to get into those mountains alive. If you leave here within an hour or so and cut straight south across country, you ought to intercept his tracks before nightfall. You can follow them on into his night camp and bushwhack the pair of them."

"What makes you think I operate that way?" Trask said, getting his back up.

Quick grinned. "Look, I don't care how you do it, and there ain't going to be any witnesses around anyway, way out there in the foothills."

"Let's see the cash."

Quick brought a poke out of his pocket and counted out five double eagles. "Half now, half when you've finished the job."

"Fair enough," said Trask as he pocketed the big coins.

"Cover your tracks," Quick advised. "Nobody'll ever know but what Buchanan and Reo got killed by Indians."

"Good idea."

"One other thing," Quick said. "Don't be in any all-fired hurry to clear out of the country after you finish the job. I may have some other chores for you. There's going to be some changes made out at Pitchfork, and there'll be a spot for you on the payroll again."

"Not so long as Mike Warrenrode's running the place, I reckon."

"Mike's getting old," Quick said meaningfully. Trask's glance came up and locked on his. Both men began to smile coolly.

Chapter Eight

JOHNNY Reo *was* humming. Finally he opened his mouth to speak. He said, "Mary Fitzsimmons from Boston, Mass., went wading in water up to her ankles."

Buchanan said, "That doesn't rhyme."

"Wait till the tide comes in," said Reo, and guffawed.

It was a desert of heroic proportions. The sun threw middle-long afternoon shadows across the baking earth. The horses carried them steadily deeper into the wilderness of rock and cactus. The plain began to wrinkle, then to heave, until their chosen route brought them down into a narrow valley bisected by the winding, tree-lined banks of a dry riverbed. Two hundred yards beyond they had to ford a shallow stream, and Johnny Reo remarked, "Rivers are as changeable as women. This creek's changed its course since those trees took root back there."

"So have we," observed Buchanan.

Reo laughed. "You know, I like the way you size up." His brash glance traveled forward toward the hills, and he said, "Gonna be a lot of Indians up there. A *lot* of Indians. We may end up playing Russian roulette with every chamber loaded."

"Every chamber but one."

"You mean old Sentos? I don't put as much trust in that old liar as you do. He's got all the character of a billy goat. Reminds me of myself, I reckon. No, Buchanan, I'd say our hill's going to get a lot higher to climb come tomorrow."

"You're a fanciful man, Johnny."

"Me? Naw."

"Then, why'd you deal yourself in?"

"For the money," Reo answered promptly. "You gotta be hard, amigo. Old Warrenrode wouldn't have got anyplace at all appealing to my conscience the way he did to yours. What's the point killing yourself for a man who doesn't even know your name?"

"I know my name," Buchanan replied.

The slopes lifted them by slow degrees. The sun quartered in at them from the right. Roundabout lay clusters of yucca and juniper; beyond stood the haze-blue risings of the saw-edged mountains, deep and thick in heavy green pine timber. But that was still many hours across the desert foothills. The middle-down sun burned their faces and hands. A jackrabbit bounded across a hillside like a kangaroo, and Reo said, "I'd feel a whole lot better about this if I knew what that girl looks like. Suppose she's three hundred pounds of ugly?"

"Then, she's lucky," Buchanan said. "If she's ugly, those young bucks won't gang up on her so fast."

"Unless she wants them to," Reo said with a sly grin. "Been my experience that a woman with her skirt up can generally run faster than a man with his pants down." He pointed ahead toward the mountains. "You been givin' any thought to how we'll handle it once we get up there?"

"Some."

"You keeping it a secret for a rainy day?"

Buchanan shrugged. "I haven't worked it out yet. How would you handle it?"

"Me? I'd go back to bed and pull the blankets up over my head."

"Then, what are you doing here?"

"I always was a sucker for money," Reo said. "Bound to be my downfall someday." He was laughing low in his throat. "Only one thing I regret. I should've held up the old man for twice as much. He'd have paid it."

"Then why didn't you?" Buchanan asked shrewdly.

"I reckon you've got more conscience than you admit to if you dig down inside deep enough."

"No," Johnny Reo said, quite grave. "Don't ever make that mistake about me, Buchanan. I never do favors. If you want true love and loyalty, there's nothing like a small dog. Don't ever start countin' on me for things money won't buy."

Buchanan glanced at him. "Suppose I don't believe you?"

"You could get yourself into a passel of grief that way." Reo built a cigarette and squinted through the smoke; he said, "I learned a long time ago how the world works. Mimbreños wiped out my folks when I was twelve, and then the puking Indians took me back to their camp and raised me. Soon as I was big enough, I took the first chance I got to run out on them. I took out across the desert on foot with a hide full of water, hiked three days into Mesilla. I was sixteen. The Mexicans in Mesilla took one look at me—I was so dirty then you couldn't even tell I had red hair—and they were about ready to scalp me for the bounty. And the whites were just as friendly. I had to run for it. I'd been three days in the desert, the last day without water, and I hadn't eaten in two days. I ran out of town down to the Rio Grande and dived in, figuring to get across. Happens the water cleaned up my hair enough, and when the Mexes caught up with me, they saw they couldn't peddle my scalp for the bounty. That's the only reason they didn't gut me right there on the river bank."

Reo's voice was flat, emotionless. He droned on: "It taught me one thing—you can't trust nobody. And it taught me another thing. How to hate. I hated Apaches and I hated Mexicans. After those Mexes let me go, I stole some food from a farmer and cut south toward El Paso. But nobody down there wanted a stringy Injun-raised kid either. I'd forgot how to talk English, pret' near. So I stole me a gun and a case of cartridges from a store down there and went across the Border. Kept practicin' and stealing more ammunition until I was as good as I figured I was going to get. Then I started huntin' Indians. They were paying fifty dollars in gold for an Apache scalp in Chihuahua. I made a pretty good pile of money. So did a lot of other gents. There wasn't no way for the Mex Government to tell the difference between the hair of an Apache and the hair of a peaceable farm Indian or even a Mex peon, for that matter. When the boys run out of Apaches to scalp, they started in on the farm towns. I guess I didn't have it in me to do that. Not then, anyhow—I still wasn't hard enough. But I learned. Knock a man down often enough, and he learns. Yes, by God."

Reo paused and pinched out the butt of his cigarette. His eyes had gone bleak; his long face had settled into grave lines. But then, abruptly, the grin flashed across his face, and he said, "Bet you're sorry for me, now. Don't be. Every word I just told you is a lie."

"I don't think so," Buchanan said.

"Then you're a bigger fool than I took you for. Why should I tell the truth to you?"

"Why shouldn't you?"

Reo laughed. "All right, have it your way. But I'll warn you of this much. When the going gets too tough, I cut and run. Don't count on me if we get in a bad pinch."

"Well, then," Buchanan said, "you might as well turn back right now."

"No. I'll bluff it out with you until I see how the land lies. Maybe you can work a deal with Sentos. Him owin' you his life and all. Maybe I can earn my five thousand without workin' for it at all. Easier that way than having Warrenrode's whole crew chasing after me."

Buchanan reined in suddenly; it forced Reo to yank his horse to a halt. Buchanan said, "In that case I think I want to be sure where you stand, Johnny. I won't go in there with you behind me unless I've got your word to hold up your end."

"That's asking a hell of a lot."

"It's that," Buchanan said, "or we split up right here. Which leaves you out here by yourself right between the Apaches and the Pitchfork crew. Make up your mind."

Reo's bony shoulders lifted two inches and dropped. "All right. You got my word. A figure of speech, of course—my word's worthless."

"I'm not so sure of that," said Buchanan. He had watched Johnny Reo make a big point out of how untrustworthy he was; Reo had made such an act of it that Buchanan wasn't inclined to believe a word of it. He liked Reo; he believed that Reo owned a bigger brand of honor than he talked.

Just the same, he intended to keep one eye on Reo at all times.

Dusk, then dark. Making no effort to conceal themselves, Buchanan and Reo beat carelessly through the night until, at the base of the higher foothills, Buchanan called a halt. "No moon tonight. Bad footing up there. We'll wait for daylight to see where we're going."

A breeze ruffled up the dying warmth of the powdered earth. Dust tickled Buchanan's nostrils. They made camp below the hill, careful to post themselves in open country surrounded by nothing more threatening than occasional clumps of scrub oak and piñon. Buchanan scooped depressions in the earth for hip and shoulder and lay down to sleep after Reo said, "I'll take first watch."

He came awake all at once, with all his fibers alert; he did not move. He heard the soft run of Reo's voice, intended to reach no farther than his ears: "Buchanan—you awake?"

"I am now."

"Look easy, amigo. Don't move. Relax and don't lift your head. We got company up on the hill."

Buchanan had gone to sleep with his six-gun in his

hand. His thumb slowly curled over the hammer; that was the only motion he made. Reo said, "They're gettin' set. I count three. Two up on the hill and one back out on the flats, about a hundred yards. Squattin' behind that big ball juniper. You got it placed in mind?"

"Yes."

"He's yours, then."

Buchanan said, "Better get ready to move, now. They look like Indians?"

"No. White men. Spotted a bandanna and chaps on one of 'em."

That was strange. But there wasn't time to ponder it. Buchanan's muscles tensed. "I'm going for the piñon. Don't bump into me."

"Going the other way," Reo murmured. "Now?"

"*Now*."

He rolled, overturning twice, flattening against the ground in the heavy shadow of the thick little piñon— and as he made his move the hard, flat echo of a rifle shot slammed across the night. A bullet clipped up dirt close by his heels and ricocheted into the sky.

The shot's echoes still rolled out when Buchanan's attention was whipping out along the flats, narrowing toward the ball juniper Reo had spotted for him. Buchanan's gun roared and bucked in his fist.

On the hill two rifles opened up in harsh signals. Their bullets churned down into the camp. Buchanan blasted three quick shots forward, all of them chewing low through the juniper; then he dived to the side and rolled to the next bush. Just in time. Seeking the point where Buchanan's muzzle flame had appeared, half a dozen shots from up above whacked cruelly into the piñon he had only just deserted.

Buchanan fired. He heard a scream from the juniper. He fired again and had the grim satisfaction of hearing the man's cry cut off in its middle. A figure flopped out onto the ground beside the juniper.

Rolling among the bushes, Buchanan found a new spot of cover shielded from the gunners up above. He plugged fresh cartridges into his revolver and caught the quick orange stab of a rifle's muzzle flash upslope. He let go on that target, and heard the loud, angry crang of ringing metal. The next shot fired from that point was fired by a six-gun. Buchanan's bullet must have smashed the rifle.

He heard the loud popping of Reo's gun and saw its scattered flashes well to his left; Reo was moving back and forth rapidly, never targeting himself. Back in the brush the hobbled horses were beginning to make a racket. The rifle uphill was going hard, methodically raking the brush with fire, and Buchanan spread himself thin to the ground. He raised his sights on the muzzle flash and let go. The bullet, deflected by some intervening branch, screamed harmlessly off.

Buchanan impatiently gathered himself and made a run for a hump of ground thirty yards ahead. Dodging and zigzagging, he made the slope with bullets plowing creases in the sand all around his boots. He belly-flopped against the uptilted ground, concealed by the ground-hump from both gunners, and crawled upward toward the crest.

Reo's laugh rang through the night; then Reo's gun quit firing, and the only shots were a ragged aftervolley from the higher rifle, which presently subsided for lack of target. In the sudden silence Buchanan inched uphill with his head turned to one side so that he could catch on the flats of his eardrums any slight sounds that might come down from above.

In time he heard the crunching of a man's boots; Buchanan lifted his head two inches and poked his gun forward. He could see the man coming down, crouching, a vague shadow drifting forward. Then Johnny Reo's voice shot forward from a point not far away on the hill. "All right, friend. Let's get it done."

The crouching figure stopped, and Buchanan could hear his breathing. The man's head swiveled around, searching the night, trying to find Reo.

"You're rigged for a cross fire. Freeze. Drop the gun," Buchanan said.

There was no motion for a moment; and then the ambusher broke and started running back up the hill, breaking the quiet with the pounding of carelessly thrown shots. Buchanan leveled his gun deliberately, but then Reo's six-gun roared twice, and the ambusher turned from his rushing course, turned as if to walk away; his high shape jerked once and fell.

Johnny Reo's soft laughter floated across the hill. "One more to go, Buchanan. What do you say we carve him up in halves, one for each of us?"

A new voice rolled downhill. "You'll have fun tryin' that, pilgrim." That was Trask's voice, full of anger and impossible to mistake. "I've hung tougher men than you two out to dry."

Buchanan knew better than to speak again. By turning his head while Trask spoke, he had a fair idea of where Trask was on the hill. He began to work his way forward and then stopped, hearing the soft brush of footsteps approaching from his left. He swung the gun around and caught Reo's lanky silhouette vague against the stars; he said, "Make more noise when you walk, Johnny," in a gentle whisper.

Trask roared, "I'm going to kill the both of you, one bullet at a time!"

Reo replied hotly, "You're burying yourself with your mouth, Trask."

And that was a mistake. Placing Reo by the sound of his voice, Trask fired. Buchanan plainly heard the *thwack* of the bullet, a soft thump heeled by the thunder of the shot and the stab of orange muzzle flame from higher along the hillside. Buchanan thumbed three shots in answer and rammed forward, butting Reo, knocking Reo down.

"Where'd he hit you?"

"I dunno." Reo sounded confused. "I don't think he hit me at all."

"I heard something."

"Yeah, so'd I." Reo rolled around on the ground, feeling his legs and back. "Nothing—wait a minute, they's a slice chewed out of my gun belt! That's all. Jesus! Guess I'm all right."

"Then, you're lucky," Buchanan whispered. "Don't let him hear you again. He's got good ears."

"And he shoots like a wizard," Reo said. He cursed mildly and dusted himself off. "What now?"

Trask yelled an oath. Gun flame lanced out, after which his running figure emerged from the shadows and scrambled across the hillside. Buchanan fired, and knew he had missed. He said under his breath, "I want him alive, Johnny."

"What the hell for?"

"To find out whose idea this was."

"I see what you mean."

Buchanan said, "Keep him busy for a few minutes while I work up toward him. Then start moving up. Circle to the left, so I'll know where you are."

Reo nodded and laid his sights on Trask's position. Buchanan pushed off, dodging from brush clump to brush clump. Reo's gun sent out covering fire at irregular intervals, receiving the answer of Trask's shots. Buchanan meanwhile roved steadily uphill, cautiously advancing. A slight sound lifted his glance, and on the rim, for a split instant, a silhouetted figure appeared. It dropped immediately from sight; and Buchanan thought, *He's gone over the top.* He began to climb rapidly from cover to cover, gun up, eyes and ears attuned.

He heard Reo scratching uphill somewhere off to his left. Near the rim he dropped belly-flat and squirmed onto the hilltop. Trask hadn't skylined again; he had to be somewhere down the backside of the hill, possibly angling to one side or the other. The murmur of a running creek drifted up, and Buchanan could vaguely make out the thicker shadow of thicket bottoms at the foot of the hill.

Man-sized boulders were scattered across this face of
the hill. Trask might be behind any one of them.

There was one way to find out. Buchanan began
working his way down, running soft-footed from rock
to rock. He kept his head down and his gun braced
before him, ready to fire.

Either Trask was in the rocks or he might have gone
right on down into the thickets. Either way, Buchanan
couldn't play a waiting game; he didn't want Trask to
get loose. He prowled downslope deliberately, exposing
himself when he had to; he drew no fire and presently
reached the edge of the bottoms, counting on Trask to
have difficulty taking aim on a constant-moving shadow
in the deep darkness.

He was low along the edge of the thicket when the
shot roared.

He couldn't tell how close the bullet came, but he
saw the muzzle flash. He fired, deliberately shooting
wide; he launched himself to the side, breaking into a
hunched dogtrot, batting branches away from his face.
An enormous rock squatted in the thicket, a boulder
eight feet high. He gained the edge of it and began to
stalk around, and then the slightest of sounds froze
him.

A faintly visible shape came swinging up past the
rock, and Buchanan leaped. He caught Trask at chest-
level, capsizing him, carrying him backward through
the bottoms. They tumbled headfirst into a foot of
water. Buchanan had his shoulder on Trask's chest; he
fumbled for Trask's gun hand. The rolling foam of the
stream splashed Buchanan's face, into his mouth and
nostrils, and he had to throw back his head to breathe.
That was when Trask rolled beneath him. It upset
Buchanan's uncertain balance; he felt the barrel of
Trask's gun glance off his jaw, raking a thin slice of
flesh with it. Before Trask could use the gun, Buchanan
slapped down with the great slab of his hand and tore
the six-gun out of Trask's skinny fist.

Trask clawed and scrambled. Somewhere his arm

bent back a branch; it came whipping out of the dark, across Buchanan's eyes. The sudden stinging blindness overturned him into the water.

He rolled over, scraped a palm across his eyes to clear them, and saw Trask on his knees feeling in the mud bottom for his gun. Trask's arms were in water up to the shoulders; his hawk face was just above the surface. Buchanan waded in and hurled the sledgehammer of his right fist. It skimmed across the water and slammed Trask full in the face. The man didn't live who would be quite right, ever again, after that blow.

It rocked Trask's head back cruelly. He fell back on his haunches, spluttering and hawking. He raised both hands, palms forward, and husked spray out of his throat. "Okay—enough."

"Get up, then."

"Gimme a minute." The dark glisten on Trask's face was blood; his nose was smashed. He got to his feet and stood weaving with water slapping his knees. He hung there, spent.

From the creek bank Johnny Reo fired.

The bullet slammed Trask back. His hands rose to his chest; he sat down in the water.

Reo ran splashing into the bottoms. Buchanan wheeled on him and roared, "You damn fool!"

"What?"

Buchanan reached down and lifted Trask out of the water. Trask coughed weakly. Buchanan said, "Still alive."

"The light was bad for shootin'," Reo apologized.

"Help me drag him out."

They hauled Trask onto the bank. He was breathing like an overheated teakettle, ragged and wheezy. Reo struck a match. Trask's eyelids fluttered.

Buchanan said, "How you makin' it, Trask?"

"Hurts like hell. But I reckon that's one way to know I ain't dead yet."

"Maybe," said Reo, "but it ain't but a short ways to

where you're going. You've just dealt yourself out of
the game."

"You're a bastard, Reo."

Buchanan leaned close to him. "Who were those two
with you?"

"Pair of gunnies I hired for peanuts. Which is all
they was worth, I see." Trask coughed weakly. He
roused himself onto his elbows. "I hope you go right on
into that Injun camp. Because they'll roast your hides
over an anthill. You ain't got a chance."

"I make my own chances," Buchanan drawled.

"Go to hell," Trask said. His arms went slack, and
he fell back. The match went out.

Buchanan laid his hand along the side of Trask's
throat, feeling for a pulse. After a moment he shook his
head.

Reo said, "I thought he was pullin' his gun. Must
have been a reflection on the water."

"Is that a fact."

"All right," Reo said. "So I cold-decked him. I sel-
dom lose my temper except when I get mad. He got me
mad."

"No point in crying over him," Buchanan said. "It's
done."

"That's the way I always look at it," Reo agreed. He
stood up and methodically plugged empties out of his
gun.

Buchanan squatted by the dead man, frowning. The
wind touched his wet clothes; he could feel with his
cheeks the direction from which it came, warm and dry
and threatening. He looked up at Reo, graven-faced.
"Anything strike you funny about this?" he asked.

"I guess not. Why?"

"He knew we were headed for Sentos' camp."

"So?"

"He wasn't at Pitchfork when we left. He was in
town. How'd he know where we're headed?"

Reo's hands became still. "Yeah," he said.

Buchanan said, "Somebody sure enough tolled him out here after us."

"Which is something to think about," Reo murmured.

Buchanan nodded. "Bring that saddle spade and my Bible. I'll read over them."

Chapter Nine

STEVE Quick had an inborn ability to mimic manners. He stood by the sideboard with a glass in his hand, one finger stuck out and his lips pursed like a rich dude. Warrenrode rolled silently into the big room in his wheelchair, catching Quick by surprise; but if Warrenrode noticed Quick with his private stock of whisky, he gave no sign of it. His look was dry, barren; his shoulders were straight and his voice curt.

"No word?"

"Not a thing."

"Jesus," Warrenrode cried. Quick could see how much graver he had become, how much more beaten down. It was waiting that did that—waiting and silence and not knowing. Quick's lip began to curl with secret contempt.

The kitchen door opened. He watched Antonia enter, her skin the color of bronze, heavy breasts bubbling under the thin cotton dress. She said, "Where've you been? I've waited supper for you."

"I had a chore in town," Quick said.

"It could've waited, couldn't it?" Warrenrode snapped. "You were needed around here today."

"What for? To join the mourning crowd?"

Warrenrode's head turned slowly, heavily like a tired lion's. He glared at Antonia. "Maybe love makes a

woman blind, but it sure seems to make you see a lot
more in this cowboy than I do."

Quick's lips pinched into a thin, pale line, but he
didn't say anything. Warrenrode prowled toward the
back of the house, thrusting the wheels of his chair with
powerful, impatient rolls of his big shoulders. Before he
disappeared into the corridor, he said, " 'Tonia."

"What?" Her answer was sullen.

"Stay tough," Warrenrode muttered. "Don't ever get
sentimental." He rolled himself out of the room. The
door slammed.

Antonia said, "What was that supposed to mean?"

"Nothin'. Don't pay him no mind. He's all busted to
pieces."

"You want to eat?"

"Sure, why not?"

Quick followed her into the kitchen and sat down.
He watched her put food in front of him. She took the
seat across the table. Quick picked at the steak. "What
I need is a drink, that's what I need."

"You just had one." He pushed his plate aside and
cursed. Antonia said, "Why are you staring at me?"

"You know."

"Someday I'd like to get inside that clever little brain
and find out what you really think."

"I'm thinking I used to like to leave my women
where I found them."

"You want me to bawl?" she said. "Nobody's keeping you here."

"No," he said. "I ain't runnin' out this time. I won't
start at the bottom. I been there, and it's too crowded."

"What a shame."

He said, "Don't get high and mighty with me,
querida. You want to eat beans the rest of your life?
You need me as bad as I need you."

She reached across the table. "Do you mean that,
Steve? Do you love me?"

Eyes at odds with his lips, Quick made a smile.
"You're a lot of woman, 'Tonia." He got up and walked

around the table, lifted her to her feet, and kissed her. Her lips were still and stiff under his; he said, "What's the matter?"

"I never know when to believe you."

Mainly he felt indifference; but he made his voice sound earnest. "What have I got to do to prove I love you?"

"I don't know," she said. "Get me out of this dismal place for a start."

"Not yet," he said.

"Then, when, Steve?"

"When we've got what we want. When we're ready."

"Suppose I don't want to wait?"

"You'll wait," he said coolly.

"Nobody ever crosses you, do they, Steve?"

"Not more than once."

She said, "Sometimes I get scared of you."

"You got nothing to be scared of, long as you play my game, querida." He touched the points of his trivial mustache and added, "Calm down. Have I ever let you down?" He turned toward the back door." Get your hat."

"What for?"

"We're riding into town. To the preacher's house."

She didn't say anything, and he looked back at her. He said, "Your mouth's open."

"But, Steve, I——"

"Get your hat," he said again. "I'll meet you down front." He went out into the night, tramped along the outside of the house to the front yard, and saw a cowboy just entering the bunkhouse. Quick yelled at him, "Boat, cut me out two horses."

"You asked me to prove I loved you," he said. The smell of the grass was a warm spice in the night. Their horses kicked up little dry balls of dust from the road. Stars sparkled on the surface of the sky, and a coyote yapped on a hill.

"It's so sudden," Antonia said in a small voice. "Steve, I'm not sure we ought to——"

"Forget it," he said. "I got to copper my bets, don't you see?"

"What do you mean?"

"Everything's all set. The whole kit and caboodle's about to fall into our hands. You and me, querida. We got to be ready for it—we got to be married."

"You don't care about anything but that ranch."

He said, "Don't put on airs, 'Tonia."

"Maybe we ought to think about——"

"Maybe, maybe, maybe," he said angrily. "Maybe if my Ma had whiskers, she'd be my Pa. I'm sick of maybes. Look, either you go through with this, or I call off the whole deal. You won't cut much of a swath back East without two copper pennies to rub together. Or was you figuring to set up business for yourself in some flyblown room over a saloon somewheres?"

He watched her with care. She didn't have any way of knowing that it was too late to call anything off. Quick's scheme had been set in motion, and there was nothing to do now but wait for it to carry itself to the finish. But he had to marry himself into the line of inheritance before she found that out.

"How about it, querida? Last chance to make up your mind."

She said, "It's a funny thing, how you can love and hate the same man."

"You aim to go through with it?"

"Yes, Steve."

"Then let's quit arguing."

He put a smile on his mouth and reached out to grasp her hand. They rode into town that way, hand in hand. They tied up in front of the preacher's house, and Quick said under his breath, "Walk like a lady, querida."

He took her up onto the porch and banged on the door until a lamp came on inside. The preacher showed up in his night-robe and stocking cap.

Quick made his grin friendly. "Sorry to get you out of bed at this hour, Reverend."

"Not half as sorry as I am." The preacher smiled raggedly.

"We'd kind of like your services," said Quick. He looked at Antonia and swallowed a sense of panic that made him want to chuck the whole thing and run like hell.

Buchanan gave a last glance to the three fresh graves, clapped on his hat, and turned to put away his camp shovel and Bible. The first streaks of false dawn were visible eastward. Johnny Reo said, "Kind of eerie, them coyotes blowing Taps out there."

"Getting on your nerves, Johnny?"

"Naw. But I could've used some more sleep. What good's buryin' the likes of these? Waste of sweat, waste of time, if you ask me."

"I guess I didn't ask you," Buchanan said.

"When my time comes, I don't much care whether they plant me or leave me to the coyotes. I aim to have my fun before I get dead, not after."

"That so?"

"Sure," said Reo. "Life is like making footprints in a sandy beach, didn't you know that?"

"What do you mean, life's like making footprints in a sandy beach?"

"How the hell do I know what I mean? I ain't no philosopher."

Buchanan grinned. "Let's saddle up."

They had a long way to go, up into the Apache stronghold. Reo said, "Ain't no rush. Them mountains will still be there tomorrow."

"But the girl may not."

"You set a lot of store by her, for a female you ain't never even laid eyes on."

"Doesn't matter," Buchanan said. "We've still got a job to do."

Reo said while saddling his horse, "There are two kinds of men in this business of ours, Buchanan—the crazy ones and the scared ones. You ain't either kind. I don't know as I like that."

"Don't lose any sleep over it."

"I guess not."

They headed up into the foothills. Buchanan tuned his ears to the long silences of the country, estimating their meaning. Silence could mean the absence of company; and it could mean the presence of company that didn't want to be heard.

The hills heaved up, irregular and barren; it was death-hot here, with no shade against the rising sun. Buchanan dismounted and had a look at a dimly scuffed mark on the flinty ground; he added that together with the broken stems of a clump of bunch grass and said, "Maybe forty-eight hours."

"Could've been Sentos and the girl," Reo said.

"Uh-huh." Buchanan gathered the reins, climbed up, and went on ahead. The hills rolled on up, and beyond them stood the black-cut higher peaks. Whole meadows of flat rock slabs hung in the hollows. Buchanan's big frame was slouched loosely, saving its energy. The hat cut low across his sun-blackened cheekbones.

Reo scraped his long, rawboned jaw. "We could get killed, you know that?"

"Warrenrode won't like that."

"I'll take a pretty dim view of it myself," said Reo. "Don't reckon I can collect the rest of that gold from the grave. Hell, Buchanan, you sure you don't know where to find Sentos?"

"Don't have to know. Once we get up in the peaks, he'll find us."

"Unless some other outfit finds us first. More'n one Injun camp up there."

"Uh-huh," Buchanan muttered with half his attention. His wary eyes absorbed the details around him. Saddle leather squeaked dryly. An earth-colored lizard sat sleepy-eyed in the minuscule shade of a hat-sized rock. Buchanan examined all those shadows and all the clumps of catclaw and Spanish bayonet—every shadow big enough to hold a solitary Indian who could lie with great patience for hours without moving. The slopes lay dust-silent under the heavy beat of the sun, the color of an old sow's belly. Reo said, "Getting to be a god-damned hot climb."

The rocks reflected heat like furnace walls. A sun-maddened scorpion rolled on the ground, stinging itself to death. Reo's horse grunted and dodged away from it.

Reo said, "Maybe we ought to cut south and angle in at them."

"No. We want them to know where we're heading."

"Yeah, but who's 'them'? Sentos has got a bunch of Mimbreños, maybe, but we're likely to find Chiricahuas up there too."

Buchanan made no answer. They swung up a steep slope, paused to blow the horses, and threaded a rocky fissure. They nooned on a hilltop, in plain view of the surrounding hills—much to Reo's disgust—and after-ward walked their horses into the crosscanyons. Buchanan's shirt was sweat-pasted skintight against his back.

By late afternoon there were a few scattered pines; the air was thinner, the heat not so brassy, and Reo was in a better mood. "Maybe find some water up here."

"Take a breath," Buchanan said, "and it tastes clean, like nobody's ever breathed the air before. I like this country."

"Now, if only it liked you."

Buchanan looked sharply left, where he thought he had seen a blur of motion slipping from one tree to another. Reo said easily, "Squirrel."

"Squirrel now, maybe, but it'll be an Apache later," Buchanan said. "We're closing in."

"Won't be too long," Reo agreed.

Sundown. Blue twilight trickled down the mountain slopes. They were on a forested slope. Buchanan said, "We'll camp here."

"Smart. Go banging around up here after dark, and no telling who might take a shot at us."

"You never know," Buchanan agreed. "Might even run into somebody friendly."

"Nothing's friendly out here."

"You need a little more faith, Johnny," Buchanan said.

"Easy for you to say. Sentos may be your friend, but he ain't mine."

"Then, think about this—if they kill you, they won't want to leave me alive to talk about it."

"Now, that does cheer me up," Reo said.

They pitched dry camp, and Buchanan moved through the trees laying down ropes. He took his time; it was an hour before he had set all his snares; and afterward he rolled out his blankets, stuffed them with hat and wadding, and joined Reo in the trees. It was full dark, starlight filtered only vaguely down through the pines. Reo murmured, "A lot of work. Suppose an Injun don't show up?"

"They're about as likely not to show up as a corpse at its own funeral."

"Now," Reo observed, "there's one hell of a lot of comfort in that thought."

In the dark the silence of the mountains seemed greater. Buchanan crouched with his head pushed against a tree trunk, hoping to pick up the rumor of vibration if anyone should approach. He noticed how taut Reo's body was; Reo had one hand on the butt of his gun. For all his studied casual deviltry, Reo was fine-tuned.

Buchanan considered the night, the forest, and the snares he had set. His battle-scarred face displayed candid good nature. "I feel hospitable. Hope we get a visitor or two."

"You never can tell," said Reo.

"I think we'll have company tonight," Buchanan said. "Spread out some to the left there. We'll see if we can't hire ourselves a guide or two. And Johnny . . ."

"What?"

"I keep remembering how you shot Trask."

"Don't worry, I ain't got the itch right now."

"That's good. Because dead Indians won't do us any good."

"*Enju*," Reo said dryly, the word being a noncommittal Apache grunt that could mean just about anything you wanted it to mean. He drifted to one side and was swallowed by the shadows.

Buchanan sat with his elbows on his knees. He took out his long-bladed sheath knife and held it with care by the blade to keep the metal from throwing a reflection. His lips formed a soundless whistle; a cheerful tune ran through his head. Thick silence had settled down in the gloomy timber corridors.

He looked across to Reo, who was only visible because Buchanan knew where to look for him. Reo had his hand on his gun; that made Buchanan frown a little. Then Reo lifted his hand to push back his hat and did not touch his gun afterward.

Searching the forest slowly, Buchanan discovered stealthy movement below and to his left. Buchanan's attention narrowed like a cone, until the whole focus of it lay against the shifting shadow.

It became an Apache, moving afoot through the trees, half-crouched, armed with a hand-axe. Buchanan's glance held on him long enough to be sure of the identification; then Buchanan shifted his eyes, moving his head ever so slightly to make sure Reo had spotted the approaching Apache. Reo squatted motionless; the way his head was set indicated he was watching the Indian. Buchanan swept the rest of the timber with his eyes and ears but discovered no other movement. He returned his attention to the lone Apache.

Buchanan's right arm dropped close to the ground, and the point of the knife blade settled against a tight-stretched rope at his feet. He held the knife there, poised and ready to cut, and watched the Indian rise from his crouch to search the night.

Presently the Apache hunkered down again and came forward, approaching near enough for Buchanan to hear the faint abrasion of his moccasins on the ground.

Two paces more, Buchanan thought. His hand tightened on the knife. The Indian halted; he stood slowly turning his head, as if he smelled trouble. He held his position for a long time, not stirring, and in the corner of his vision Buchanan could see a tiny movement—it might have been Reo's hand curling around his gun butt. But at that moment the Apache moved, advancing alertly, right foot and then left foot . . .

Buchanan's knife slashed down. The keen edge sliced through the hemp cord. A thick, bent sapling sprang upright. Suspended from it was a loop of rope that lifted smartly around the Apache's ankles, flipped the Indian over, and hung him dangling by his feet, with his head two feet off the ground.

Reo chuckled happily. The Indian grunted. Buchanan rushed forward and chopped the blade of his big hand down, dislodging the war axe from the Apache's grip.

Reo came up, squatted down, and laughed. "How about that?"

The Indian's face looked odd upside down. He opened his mouth and let out an ear-splitting bellow.

Buchanan nodded. "All right. Every Apache within five miles heard that."

"It's a hard life," Reo sighed. He tugged a short length of rope out of his belt and made a grab for the Indian's wrists. Buchanan swung forward to help.

When they had the Indian's hands tied, they let him down to earth. Reo said, "Aravaipa Apache. Ain't none of Sentos' boys."

"Too bad, then," said Buchanan, "but he'll do."

The Indian watched all this with a baleful sullen glare, unblinking. Reo suddenly unleashed a torrent of guttural Apache words at him. The Indian listened impassively and grunted three or four syllables in answer.

Buchanan said, "Have to do better than that."

"Uh-huh," Reo said. "Lend me that toad-sticker."

"Careful how you handle it."

"Sure," Reo said. He accepted the knife hilt-first and turned toward the Indian, who watched without expression. Reo laid the edge of the knife against the Indian's Adam's apple. It rested there of its own weight. Reo spoke softly. The Indian said nothing.

Buchanan said, "Remind him what happens to his spirit if he gets killed at night."

"He knows all that, I reckon."

Reo's hand stirred. A trickle of blood appeared at the Apache's throat. Reo lifted the knife and turned it from side to side. "Pain don't scare them none, but he'll think a couple minutes about spendin' eternity in the Happy Huntin' Ground in darkness. He'll come around."

The Indian came around. He began to talk sullenly. Buchanan listened, getting the gist of it.

Reo interpreted. "Says to tell him what we want of him."

"Ask him if he knows where Sentos is."

"He does."

"Tell him we want to see Sentos. Tell him we want him to take us there."

Some Apache talk rattled back and forth. Afterward Reo said, "He ain't partial to the idea."

"Doesn't matter," Buchanan said. "We'll use him as a hostage. We won't get far before Sentos will find us. The trick is to keep to open country, where they can't jump us."

By first light they moved out, penetrating the mountains. Buchanan picked open hilltops and wide ridges to travel. The Indian walked between them at the center of a rope that ran from Buchanan's saddle to Reo's. Now and then the Indian turned his head and spat. He had no other comments.

Buchanan kept his rifle balanced across his saddle horn. All morning he'd had a feeling like ice across the back of his neck and he made no argument when Reo observed, "Here we are riding along like Custer . . ."

There was no more talk until half past nine by the sun, when Buchanan halted his horse on a razorback ridge and eased his seat in the saddle. Reo drew up alongside, and the Indian stood between them, steadfastly staring at the ground as if there were some fascinating object two feet in front of his moccasins.

"Here we are," Buchanan said.

Reo nodded. "It worked. Not that I take any particular joy from it."

Coming up the ridge toward them were six Indians on horseback. They all looked like wooden cigar-store figures, for all the expression they gave. Two of them wore faded blue shirts, tails out, over buckskin leggings. The others were stripped down to hunting dress—breechclout and headband, barefoot and bareback.

"Sentos' tribe markings," Reo said. "But I don't see Sentos in the bunch."

"Don't get nervous with your trigger finger until we find out how they want to play the game," Buchanan said.

"Hell of a time to tell a man not to get nervous."

Buchanan let the rifle lie in the notch between pommel and gun belt; he lifted both hands empty into plain sight and held up his right hand palm-forward. It was supposed to be a sign of peace, but it took two parties to make peace, and he didn't have a great deal of confidence in the gesture. Still, what encouraged a man was that the six Indians yonder were riding forward in a bunch, in plain sight, and in no evident hurry.

The captive Indian looked up at Reo and said something in a very dry voice. Buchanan said, "What'd he say?"

"Says our heads are as empty as his belly."

"Could be right," Buchanan said. "But those six look friendly enough."

"When a cougar bares his fangs, it don't pay to assume he's smiling," said Reo.

The six Indians rode to a point fifty feet away and stopped. Reo murmured, "Raiding party—otherwise they'd be on foot. And by the way, I hope you've taken a look over yonder." Reo nodded toward the west.

Buchanan had already seen it—the unraveling dust plume of a single rider galloping toward them at the far end of the mile-long ridge.

One of the six Apaches detached himself from the bunch and rode forward. He drew rein ten feet from Buchanan and said, "*Enju.*"

"Sure;" Buchanan said. "*Enju.* You're Matesa, I remember you."

"Buchanan," said Matesa, and nodded. He had a face that looked as though a woodpecker had used it for target practice. Most Apaches were sawed-off and squat, but Matesa was about Ben Scarlett's size—some bigger than Buchanan, which made him bigger than big. Buchanan hadn't been in Sentos' camp for quite a spell, but it was hard to misplace the recollection of an outsized Apache with a face like Matesa's.

The trouble with Matesa, Buchanan recalled, was that his personality was a match for his looks. Matesa would fight at the drop of a hat and would drop the hat himself.

Matesa's thick arm swept toward the captive Apache, helplessly roped between Buchanan and Reo. Matesa said, "What you got him for?"

"To keep us alive," Buchanan said.

Matesa shrugged elaborately. When his great rippling muscles all settled back into place, he said, "That one Aravaipa. Don't matter dead or not. Would you carry a war shield with hole in it?"

"Better that than no shield at all," said Buchanan.

Matesa grinned. His teeth pointed in several directions, and his grin was only slightly less unsettling than his frown. He said, "I have not killed Aravaipa in many suns."

"You'll have to kill me too, then."

"No trouble," Matesa said. "I kill you slow, Buchanan. I don't forget the handkerchief fight."

Matesa turned to look over his shoulder. Buchanan said, "Before you turn them loose on us, maybe you'd better talk to Sentos first."

"Sentos not here," Matesa said with indisputable logic.

"Then ask *him*." Buchanan was pointing toward the hard-riding horseman who was just then emerging from his own dust cloud on the ridge.

Matesa shrugged again. "Matesa asks no one. A warrior asks no one."

"Maybe," Buchanan said, and watched the new-comer rein his horse down and swirl into the center of things. This was Cuchillo, the surviving son of old Sentos. Cuchillo reached out and gripped Buchanan's arm in the Indian handshake. Buchanan exchanged greetings and said, "Better tell your friend here to take us into camp before he carves us up."

Cuchillo turned and spoke rapidly to Matesa. The big brute listened expressionlessly and then laid his fist against his chest. "This *my* war party."

Cuchillo shook his head and spoke again. After a moment Matesa growled, clamped his mouth shut, and wheeled his horse around. His arm whipped up and down, and he went drumming down off the ridge at a dead run. The five bucks streamed away after him.

Johnny Reo said, "Think of that, now."

Buchanan nodded. "We got this far, anyway."

Cuchillo said, "You have given our lives to my father and to me. You will be honored in our village."

Honored, Buchanan thought, *but watched*. He said, "Let's go, then."

The grin Reo gave him was bleak and very, very dry.

Chapter Ten

THE Aravaipa went his own way, rubbing his rope-burned wrists and staring fixedly at Buchanan and Reo as if to burn their faces indelibly into his memory. They watched him tramp out of sight. Cuchillo led them down into the timber, where the trees closed in on them and they had to ride single file through the cool, dark corridors of pine. There wasn't much talk. Cuchillo seemed happy enough, but the white man hadn't been born who would have felt calm and easy just then. Buchanan kept his eyes open and his rifle handy. An Apache on foot could cover an incredible amount of ground in a short time, and it was always possible that the Aravaipa they had insulted would find a weapon somewhere and come after them. Not to mention a few hundred other Indians who tended to shoot at any white man first and ask who he was later.

It took the rest of the morning and part of the afternoon. They climbed steadily along the slopes of wooded canyons into the deepest reaches of the mountains; in time they were close to timberline, at high altitude, where the timber began to thin out. The peaks buckled up, bald and jagged, faced with stunted shrubs. The son of Sentos kept up a steady pace. Reo said, "Maybe it's the cold, thin air up here, and then again maybe it ain't." He turned up the shirt collar around his neck.

An Indian appeared on a hill and stood watching them. It meant one thing, for sure: the Indian wasn't alone. There was no telling how many pairs of eyes were keeping them in view. Buchanan saw the dark wariness of Reo's expression. He looked up with hang-dog eyes. "Right now I'd like to give the man back his twenty-five hundred dollars and call it even."

"Scared, Johnny?"

"Ain't you?"

"Sure I am."

"A man'd have to be plumb crazy not to be scared," Reo said.

A cool current of air swept across the slope, chilling Buchanan, riffling his skin. Up front Cuchillo's black head bobbed steadily forward. They entered a district of tall rock slabs tilted at improbably balanced angles; the wind hummed a steady monotone through these acoustic chambers. Squat brown men with hair bound tight with strips of colored cloth kept appearing along the trail and standing there to watch with steady eyes.

Their horses moved along the floor of a long canyon. Indians began to drift down toward them, taking positions and walking along with them; in fifteen minutes there was an escort of a dozen Apaches on foot. One of them made a joke, and the others laughed. Reo said, "I hope Sentos is in a good mood too."

They broke out of the canyon, walking their horses, and soon, on the side of a mountain that commanded a large district, Cuchillo brought them into the rancheria. It was a sprawling scatter of wickiups, spread without pattern along the humps and hollows of the mountainside. A thin stream ran down the foot of the slope. The ranks of the pedestrian escort were swelled by thirty or forty children who fell in and marched along, staring curiously at the two white men. Old women came out of the wickiups and glared defiantly at Buchanan and Reo; one woman picked up a handful of dirt and flung it. Reo dodged, and the dirt flew harmlessly past. A flung rock hit Buchanan in the thigh; he ignored it.

A gray woman came out of a wickiup, and abruptly one of the Indian braves wheeled and ran away into the rocks. Reo grinned. "Must've been his mother-in-law. A man ain't supposed to look at his mother-in-law."

They reached the chief's lodge. Cuchillo stopped.
Reo said, "Better not step down until we're invited."
"Yes."

Stooping to clear the low doorway, Sentos came into
view. Under the brim of his stovepipe hat, the old
Indian's face was a map of seams and creases. It broke
into a broad grin, and Buchanan said, "We can get
down now."

A woman came forward with obvious intent, taking
the reins of the two saddle horses and standing blank-
faced while Buchanan and Reo dismounted. Sentos
looked around at the circling crowd, listened to its
noise, and nodded carefully; he indicated the doorway
of the lodge with a sweep of his arm, afterward pushing
the hung blanket aside and entering.

"After you," Reo said dryly, and followed Buchanan
into the dimness of the wickiup.

A small fire burned in the center of the place, to
keep the mountain chill away from Sentos' old bones.
Sentos sat down cross-legged on a blanket, waving his
arms toward the ground beyond the fire. "You come to
my house—good, good." Sentos' eyes were lighted by
proud pleasure.

Buchanan said in his cautious, stumbling Apache,
"May the god of the sun be kind to the great war
chief."

Sentos dipped his head in reply. Cuchillo ducked
into the place and squatted down behind his father's
left shoulder.

Buchanan kept smiling at the old chief while he said,
"Johnny."

"What?"

"See any sign of our package?"

"No."

Buchanan went right into a short speech in Apache,
a few pleasantries to accommodate the Apache code of
etiquette. He bragged some, and Sentos bragged some,
and Reo bragged too. Buchanan told a lie, and Sentos
told a bigger one, and they both laughed. It had been a

long time since Buchanan had been in an Apache lodge, and the smell was strong in his nostrils.

After twenty minutes of pipe-smoking and desultory amenities, Sentos spoke to his son, who went outside and returned shortly with a gourd. It passed from hand to hand. Buchanan swallowed a stiff slug of tulapai and felt it burn a vicious path into his gut. He handed the gourd to Sentos, watched the stovepipe hat tip back and the old man's Adam's apple bounce up and down, and said to Sentos, "Amigo, I want to take the white woman."

There followed Sentos' short grunt. His black eyes shifted from the jug to Reo, to Cuchillo, finally to Buchanan. He grunted again. "She is your woman?"

"She's my woman," Buchanan lied. It was a subterfuge he and Reo had decided on; it was about the only thing he could think of that might work.

Sentos studied Buchanan's face. After a while he said, "She talks only about the one with bad legs."

"Her father."

"Only about him. She does not talk about Buchanan." Then, abruptly, the old man got to his feet and left the wickiup. Cuchillo went out after him.

It left Buchanan and Reo alone inside. Reo shifted forward and spoke in a tone that carried no farther than Buchanan's ears. "I don't think he bought it."

"It's the kind of lie where he knows I'm lying, and he knows I know he knows it. But he owes me his life and he's not about to call me a liar to my face."

Reo shook his head. "Buchanan, we're hanging on by a hair. He's probably talking to the girl right now. When he finds out she's never even heard of you, both our heads are going to roll right into the basket."

"No," Buchanan said. "He'll be talking to his subchiefs right about now, finding out whether they're willing to let the girl go."

"And if they ain't?"

"Then we play it by ear."

"What makes you such a goddamn hero, Buchanan? It just ain't natural. We could pull out right now and go back and tell Warrenrode his daughter's dead. Nobody'll know the difference."

"Nobody but you and me," Buchanan said. "There are things you can't stay out of."

"Aagh."

When Sentos pushed back the flap and returned into the wickiup, his face was long and guarded. He sat down and arranged his shirttails and said, "I have consulted with the spirits and with my own heart."

"A man must do that," Buchanan agreed gravely.

Sentos said, "It is truc I owe you a life, maybe two. If it was in my heart that the white woman will be killed, then I, Sentos, would say to you this—she will not be killed. But it is never in my heart to kill the white woman. And there is a thing more. When a warrior goes to steal a horse, he will use all his tricks against the man who owns the horse. This a warrior must do. And so there is no anger in my heart against you, my friend Buchanan, even though you try to trick me. When we stole the white woman from the house of the man with bad legs, my own eyes saw her in the arms of a white man with glass in front of his eyes. She is not your woman."

Buchanan said nothing. He could see Reo stiffen, out of the corner of his vision, but he sat still and only kept his eyes fixed on Sentos' eyes. The old Indian had a weazened, pickled face; he looked very sad. He made a small smile and said, "Come," and led the way outside.

As if deep in thought, Sentos led the way along an aimless path through the Apache camp. Indians lowered their eyes as he passed, in deference to the elder chieftain; but once Sentos went by, their defiant glowers lifted against Buchanan and Reo. Reo muttered, "They've got all the warm instincts of a hangman, every one of them. We better get out butts out of here."

Mescal heads roasted in a baking pit; piñon nuts and juniper berries lay on flat rocks outside wickiups. An

old man sat mending a longbow. In the shade of a
brush ramada, women in deerskins and turquoise orna-
ments squatted and sewed skins together with deer
sinew and bone awls. All this activity stopped when the
two white men came by; black eyes came up and lay
against them, unblinking and unfriendly.

Sentos brought them around the end of a wickiup
and stopped. He raised his hand to point toward a fat
man in body paint who sat in the middle of a large
cleared flat of earth. Two men sat nearby, softly beating
out rhythms on a pottery drum and a rattle made from
an eagle's claw.

"He is Lazen," Sentos explained. "The snake shaman."

Lazen, the medicine man, was reaching toward the
small fire in the center of the circle. He pulled out a
twig and held its glowing end to a ceremonial cigarette
in his mouth. When he had it going, he turned toward
the east and puffed out a ball of smoke. He turned
south and puffed out another ball of smoke. He kept
this up until he had puffed smoke in the four compass
directions, after which he opened a drawstring pouch
and set out pollen in the same four directions around
him. The colored pollen followed the Apache tradition
of hues: black to the east, blue to the south, yellow to
the west, and white to the north.

Buchanan knew enough about Apache ceremonies to
know that this was the beginning of an important one.
He also knew that old Sentos wouldn't have brought
him around to see this unless he had a reason.

The pottery drum made an insistant clatter. Small
clusters of hunters and women drifted toward the circle
and stood around, watching the medicine man perform
his rituals. The fire grew—everyone who came brought
fuel to throw on it—and at intervals the shaman tossed
powder into the fire that made bright-hued smoke shoot
up.

Sentos motioned with his finger and stepped eight or
ten paces away from the gathering circle of Indians.

When Buchanan and Reo came over, Sentos spoke in a drone.

"Before the sun sets, there will be a ceremonial tipi of four sticks. There will be songs and drinking and dance and a feast. It is the ritual of White Painted Woman."

Reo gave him a curious look and said to Buchanan, "Puberty rite for some girl."

Sentos said, "The rite of the maiden. She is older than our own, your white woman, Buchanan. But no woman in the Apache tribe can be married to a warrior unless she has come of age according to the dance of White Painted Woman." Sentos said it casually, so that Buchanan would know it was important.

Buchanan said, "You figure to marry her off?"

"She will marry a warrior tomorrow when the sun is highest."

"What if she doesn't like the idea?" Reo asked.

Sentos only grunted. He turned and poked his bony finger against Buchanan's high chest. "My friend Buchanan, no harm will come to the white woman. But she will be the wife of a brave."

"And then?"

"A few moons will pass, and she will carry a warrior's child. And when she has slept on an Apache warrior's pallet for that long, then she will be sent back to the white man with bad legs."

Buchanan's glance whipped around to Reo's. Reo's face was drawn and quietly angry. It was a cruel and brutal insult Sentos intended—to fill Marinda Warrenrode's belly with an Apache's baby and then dump her back on her father's doorstep.

Sentos in his way was a wily match for old Warrenrode. Nothing he could do to Warrenrode's daughter could hurt Warrenrode as much as this.

Sentos said, "The one with bad legs has killed two of my sons, Buchanan." He picked up a scratching stick and rubbed it up and down his back. "He will have his daughter returned to him. You can tell him this, from

Sentos. When the snow comes to the foothills, when the birds have flown to Mexico and the snakes sleep in bands, then he will have his daughter back."

Buchanan said, "It's a wrong thing to do, amigo. If you hate a man, then you should fight him. But a man who fights another man's woman is not as much of a man as I always thought Sentos was." He laid the full force of his ice-blue gaze against Sentos.

Sentos shook his head. "You are a brave man, Buchanan, but you are not Apache and you do not know the Apache way."

"I know this much. If you do this to Warrenrode, you'll make an enemy who will spend forty years hunting you if he has to. He'll kill every Apache he sees. He'll blame all Indians for what one Indian has done, and his men and his guns will give you no peace."

Sentos shrugged. "Your white-eyed soldiers have tried. If they cannot trap the Apache, then I do not fear the man with bad legs."

Sentos began to turn; then he swung back toward Buchanan and said in a very quiet voice, "He will hurt the way I have hurt. He will feel as I have felt—that he has knives sticking in his body."

The old man threw down the scratching stick. He added, "You are my guests in the rancheria, and I am happy that you stay as long as you wish—eat my food, drink my drink, smoke my pipe, and accept the honor of the Apache village. But there will be no more talk of the white woman."

With that, Sentos tramped away with stiff and choppy strides.

Buchanan said, "You can't help seeing the old man's point."

"That's exactly what I say," Reo agreed eagerly. "Now, let's just mosey on over and pick up our horses and make tracks out of here while the old bastard's still in a good mood."

"No," Buchanan said. "We'll take the girl with us when we go."

"You're joking."

Buchanan shook his head. "Honest to God, Johnny."

"Maybe you better count me out, then," Reo said, and turned to walk away.

Buchanan said gently, "I wouldn't do that, was I you."

It stopped Reo and turned him around. "Why not?"

"I'm your ticket home," Buchanan said. "You don't mean a thing to these Indians. Long as you're under my wing, you're guaranteed safe conduct. But light out on your own, and you'll have every Apache in the mountains on your track."

Reo lifted his finger. "We take the girl out of here, and we'll have them on our track anyway."

"All right, then. Suit yourself. But it's going to get mighty lonesome out on that trail come nightfall."

Reo considered it. "Yeah," he muttered, "I see what you mean." He looked up. "You're a number one son of a bitch, you know that?"

"Me?" said Buchanan. "I'm just a peaceable man." He tugged his hat down and sent his glance around slantwise, from hut to hut. "Let's see if we can find the girl."

Chapter Eleven

THEY *found her* but only at a distance. Three sturdy-looking Apaches with rifles barred Buchanan's way. He caught the reckless gleam in Reo's eye. Reo was all ready to draw his gun, but Buchanan shook his head and said in a soft voice, "Can't gunfight the whole tribe, Johnny."

And so they stood there, trying to look innocent, and the three Apaches stood there, trying to look tough, and beyond the three Apaches the hill sloped down to where the creek ran by, and there worked a number of squaws, some of them wearing their infant children in cradleboards on their backs. Tramping around in knee-high moccasins, they tended a sparse cornfield by the creek. Farther along, three women crouched pulling up the root stocks of tule plants. And that was where Buchanan saw Marinda Warrenrode.

It was impossible to mistake her. No one had given her clothes; she wore a cotton blouse and skirt, or what was left of them. But it was her hair that made her easy to recognize so far away. Blonde as flax. The kind that seemed as white and fragile as corn tassels in the spring.

She was standing with her mouth clamped shut and her arms folded under her breasts, staring resolutely straight ahead and paying absolutely no attention to the abuse the squaws shouted at her. One of the squaws walked by and slammed a stick against Marinda's arm and kept right on walking. Marinda didn't stir. After a moment Buchanan saw why: her feet were tied together.

"Hobbled like an animal," he breathed, and glanced at Reo.

If Reo was offended, he gave no sign of it. All he said was, "She's lucky if that's all they've done to her."

Buchanan said, "I've got to get close enough to talk to her."

"I wish you a lot of luck," said Reo very dryly. He grinned brashly at the three Apache riflemen who stood across his path. One of them grinned back—and drew back the hammer of his Springfield to full cock.

Buchanan said, "You heard what the old man said. Come sundown they'll be running her through their coming-of-age ceremony, and tomorrow noon she'll be married off. We've got to get her out of here before that."

"Why?"

Buchanan didn't bother to answer that. He turned his back to the three Apaches and said under his breath, "Drift on over here with me a piece." Reo rammed his hands in his pockets, acting unconcerned, and ambled along. They walked back toward the center of the village; after a few paces the three Indian riflemen fell behind, stopped, and started to talk among themselves, laughing softly. Buchanan glanced back and said, "Seems clear enough old Sentos told those three to keep us from getting close to the white girl. We've got to figure out some way to distract the three of them long enough to get a chance to talk to her."

"I'm all ears," Reo suggested.

"You might pick a fight with one of them. That'd keep them busy long enough for me to slip down to the creek."

"I'm still listening," Reo said coldly. "I ain't heard anything yet."

"Scared?"

"What do you take me for?"

Buchanan said, "I'm still trying to get that figured out, too. But right now we've got other questions to answer, and the first one is how in the hell to get a word in with the girl."

Reo squinted his eyes up into a faraway, thoughtful expression; he pinched his lips with forefinger and thumb, and said, "As I recollect, they'll put her inside an empty wickiup before the ceremony starts. A woman's supposed to have an hour or so to meditate and put childhood behind her before she goes out under the open tipi and lets the medicine man go to work on her."

"Then she'll be by herself in a wickiup?"

"If they do it the usual way. No guarantee of that, of course. Sometimes they break their own rules. This whole puberty ritual's supposed to take four days, but I reckon being as how she's white, they prob'ly decided to get it over and done with—she ain't got no mother here to stand around being proud of her."

Buchanan nodded. "Then, we'll just have to wait and

keep our eyes open and find out what hut she goes into."

"And in the meantime," Reo added, "we can see about staying alive."

Steve Quick sat brooding on the corral gate. He watched the cowhands file into the bunkhouse to lay by their hats and guns before supper, but he didn't follow them inside. Things, Steve Quick was discovering anew, had a way of going wrong just when it looked as if everything were falling neatly into place.

It had started off with Antonia. No sooner had the preacher pronounced them man and wife than Antonia had decided to tell the whole world about it. That didn't fit into Steve Quick's plans, and he'd had a tough time convincing her to keep the marriage secret. He knew she wouldn't keep her mouth shut for long.

He'd been counting on Ben Scarlett, but he could see Scarlett coming out of the cookshack now, and there was Mike Warrenrode, big as life in his wheelchair on the front stoop of the ranch house. Scarlett looked that way, grimaced, and hurried toward the corral.

Quick waited for him to come up. Quick's expression was caustic and impatient. The low-slanting sun reached in under his hatbrim and made a frizzy wisp of his mustache.

Scarlett reached the gate and looked up. It was always hard to read his face; he had a limited range of expressions. He was big and slow and hardhearted; he had been born with size but no talent, and his clumsy fighting ability was all he had to be proud of.

Scarlett said, "I went in there and told him to quit hiring people to pick on me."

"Did you."

"Warrenrode don't listen good," Scarlett complained.

"Maybe you didn't talk loud enough."

"How loud do I have to talk?"

"Loud enough so Mike Warrenrode gets dead," Steve Quick said. "It's the only way you'll stop him."

Scarlett scraped his face with his fingernails and frowned. "Race Koenig was in there."

"Race puts his pants on the same way you do. You going to let him scare you?"

"I ain't scared of nobody," Scarlett said, heating up.

Quick said coolly, "I don't believe you."

"I didn't think you would," Scarlett answered. "But you just climb down off there and mix it up with me if you think I'm so yellow."

"Pick on somebody your own size," Quick said absently. He was grinding one fist into the other palm. Scarlett, obviously, was useless as long as he didn't see a foolproof road ahead of him. It meant Quick had to make the road foolproof. He nodded, in confirmation of his own decision, and got down off the gate.

"All right," he said. "I'll go inside and tell Race to go out back, tell him I need to talk to him private-like. When you see him and me leave the house, you can go in."

"What about Antonia? What if she sees me?"

"Antonia won't give you no trouble, Ben. I can promise you that much."

"How?"

Quick sized him up. "Ben, a lot of people don't understand me. All they see is the gracious, warm surface. Let me tell you something. Underneath, I'm a first-class son of a bitch. Antonia steps out of line, I'll shove her back onto it. Don't fret none about that."

"Well," Scarlett said uncertainly.

"You got your gun loaded?"

"Yeah, sure. But I . . ."

Steve Quick didn't let him finish. He set off toward the house, figuring that if he kept things moving fast enough, Scarlett wouldn't have time to stop and work it all out with the slow machinery of his brain.

Quick saw Warrenrode back his wheelchair into the house. That was fine. That was all according to sched-

ule; Warrenrode always went inside about this time to
wash up for dinner. Scarlett might catch him alone by
the commode.

When Quick entered the house, the parlor was empty. Warrenrode had already gone into the back corridor. Quick turned to his right, into the front hall, and
had gone half a dozen paces when the door at the far
end came open, and Race Koenig's tall shape moved
into the corridor.

That was Antonia's room. Quick's eyes narrowed
down, and his mouth pinched together. Antonia appeared in the doorway behind Koenig and began to say
something. Quick tramped forward and snapped at her,
"I told you to stay away from him."

Koenig said, "She ain't your property, Steve."

Antonia said, "I told him to leave, Steve."

"For a fact," Keonig said. "Anyhow, I only wanted
to get her out to the kitchen. The old man's hungry."

"Just so that's all you wanted," Quick said. Koenig
walked past him, toward the front of the house, and
Quick stayed behind long enough to speak to the girl in
a taut whisper. "Stay inside your room and don't come
out, no matter what you hear."

"What? Steve——"

"Just stay inside," he told her. He went back down
the corridor to the parlor and said to Koenig, "Walk
out back with me, Race. Got something I want to talk
to you about."

Koenig gave him a suspicious look. Through the
half-open door Quick could see Ben Scarlett slowly
approaching in the yard. His heartbeat became more
rapid and he said, "Come on," and walked with long
strides toward the back door.

"What the hell," Koenig said, but he came. Quick
waited just outside the house, and made sure the door
was shut behind Koenig. Then he led the way toward
the windmill trough by the back barn.

Koenig said suspiciously, "What's this about, Steve?
Something on your mind?"

"It's the old man," Quick said, desperately hunting around in the recesses of his mind. He covered his confusion by building a cigarette. He was thinking of Scarlett, and the half-open front door of the ranch house, and what Scarlett—if his wits didn't desert him— was about to do. Quick's hands trembled slightly, enough to make him spill tobacco, and he made a mess of the cigarette.

"I ain't got all night," Koenig prodded.

"Look," Quick said abruptly, "what I really wanted to talk about is 'Tonia. You and me got to come to an understanding, Race. We can't all the time be sniffin' around each other like a pair of strange dogs. Now, I ain't never cut in on Marinda with you. I'd kind of like to have you pay me and 'Tonia the same courtesy. I don't reckon——"

"This is a hell of a time to mention Marinda," Koenig said. His jaw clamped tight, and he spoke through his teeth. "I've been meaning to say this to you. If you'd had any spine, you'd have ducked inside the house when those two Indians showed up. You'd have grabbed yourself a gun and cut down on the two of them. Hadn't been for you freezing up, Marinda'd never be up in that Apache camp now. So just don't you start getting on my back about 'Tonia. I've never laid a hand on her and never intend to. For all she's worth, you're welcome to her."

"Now, hold on just a minute!" Quick began, but he was cut off by the hollow boom of a gun going off inside the house.

Gunshot echoes rolled across the yard. Koenig wheeled. "What the hell?"

"How in hell should I know?" Quick said, making his eyes round with innocence.

Koenig didn't even glance at him; Koenig's legs started churning, and before Quick could move, Koenig was halfway to the house, running hard. Quick broke out of his tracks and ran after him. What ran through his mind was, *Thanks, Race, you've given me an airtight*

alibi. The back door was still swinging from Koenig's
wrenching when Quick charged through into the house.
He practically ran full-tilt into Koenig's broad back.
Koenig was standing flat-footed in the parlor, his bespectacled face swinging back and forth, trying to deter-
mine which direction the shot had come from.

A voice bellowed down the back corridor: "Goddamnit, somebody get in here!"

Quick's heart leapt into his throat. That was Mike
Warrenrode's voice.

Scarlett had slipped up, sure enough. When Quick
sidled into the old man's room, half expecting to be
shot at, he found Warrenrode unscratched, sitting in his
wheelchair with a smoking Colt .44 in his fist. On the
floor was a limp hulk that had been Ben Scarlett not
long before.

Warrenrode was breathing hard; a rime of sweat
glistened on his face, and his eyes were big and wide.
"Jesus," he growled. "Jesus."

Race Koenig knelt down by Scarlett and felt for a
pulse. Warrenrode said, "Don't bother. He was dead
when he fell. I'm still a pretty damn good shot."

"Drilled dead center," Koenig said. "I'll say you are.
What happened?"

Steve Quick held his breath and got ready to run.
Warrenrode said, "He'd been in here earlier today—
you were here. Some garbled song and dance about
how he wanted his old segundo's job back and how he
thought I'd hired Buchanan to beat him up and scare
him out of the country."

Steve Quick said carefully, "How'd he get that idea
in his head?"

"Search me," Warrenrode said. His breathing was
settling down. He made a face and put his gun away in
the holster under the blanket that covered his legs. "He
came in here like a ten-wheel locomotive just now.
Yelled something about me trying to get him killed,
and went for his gun."

Warrenrode added, "Ben never was worth a hoot with a gun."

Quick allowed himself to start breathing regularly again. At least Scarlett hadn't revealed the truth. Quick's plan was still secret. Now all he had to do was persuade Antonia to keep her stupid mouth shut until he'd had time to work up a new scheme to do away with Warrenrode.

Rushing in from the yard, the Pitchfork hands began to crowd into the hall. Steve Quick melted back into the crowd, pushed his way through, and went across the parlor to the front hall. Nobody paid any attention to him. A chorus of excited talk ran back and forth through the milling cowhands. Quick went back down the front hall and knocked on Antonia's door and when she opened it, he slipped inside and closed it behind him.

He said, "Ben Scarlett made a play for the old man and fouled it up. The old man killed him."

"Ben Scarlett?" she said. "I don't understand."

"You don't need to," he said. "The point is——"

"You hired Scarlett," she broke in. "Now I see. You put Scarlett up to it. You didn't have the nerve to do it yourself, did you?"

"Why should I take a chance like that?" he demanded. "No sense in putting my own neck in a noose if anything went wrong."

Her mouth pouted at him. She went across the room to the bed and sat down. She said irrelevantly, "You didn't even sneak in to see me last night—and here we are married!"

"For Christ's sake," he said, exasperated.

"I'm going to tell him," she said. "I'm going to tell all of them we're married. Then we can sleep together like respectable married people."

"Soon," he said, trying to placate her. "Soon, querida, but not just yet. Hell, it'll have to be soon—it won't be long before that preacher in town spreads the word all over the valley."

"Then, why can't we tell them now?" she demanded.

"Because," he said, with all the patience he could muster, "once the old man finds out about us, he'll start putting two and two together and he'll start asking himself a question or two. He might even go down to see that lawyer in town and have a look at his last will and testament. And we can't afford to let him do that."

"You'll just have to kill him first," Antonia said. "It won't work to pawn the job off on somebody else, Steve. You tried that with Scarlett. You'll have to do it yourself."

"Ain't much love lost in this family, is there?"

"Not enough to get lost," she answered. "Don't pretend you're shocked, Steve. We both know that the only time Mike Warrenrode can do either one of us any good is when he's dead. Why beat around the bush?"

He said, "Remind me never to turn my back on you."

Her smile was thin and cool. "I'll do that, husband. Now, what about it?"

He nodded. "I'll do it."

"Right away," she said.

"No. I got to think it out, how to do it. But it'll be soon. Tonight, maybe. We can't let it hang fire any longer. But by Christ I'd feel a lot better if I'd had some word from Trask."

"Don't wait," she said. "Get it done."

Quick brought up his eyes to meet hers. He studied her across a broken interval of time, at the end of which he said, "I reckon you're right."

CHAPTER TWELVE

HALF a dozen half-naked brown youths played stickball in the gathering twilight. Buchanan stood with his shoulder tipped against the trunk of a lone pine, watching with his eyes half shuttered. A clean-gnawed legbone of a wren hung in his fist.

Johnny Reo sauntered forward from the center of camp, elaborately nonchalant. "Had enough to eat?"

"Until next time," Buchanan said.

Reo gazed out at the Apache youths, who had paused in their game to stare at him balefully. He muttered, "Sticks and stones can break my bones, so I wish they'd put them down."

Within a few moments the boys tired of staring. They resumed their game—hurling a deer-hide ball from paired sticks toward the wooden silhouette of a fish at the top of a lodgepole. When a thrower missed, a boy on the far side of the pole was supposed to catch the ball between his two long sticks. Reo said, "They're faster'n hell and they've got good eyes. Don't think I'd like to meet them when they've growed up."

"Uh-huh," Buchanan said. "What'd you find out?"

Reo had to throw his head back to look at Buchanan; Reo was tall enough, but Buchanan was oversized. Reo said, "I made a right guess. They took the girl into that wickiup behind Sentos' lodge."

"Alone?"

"Looks like."

Buchanan said, "Tell me something, Johnny. You ever seen the Apache puberty ceremony?"

"Yep."

Buchanan nodded. "So have I. I'd just as soon she didn't have to go through it."

"Meaning?"

"Meaning I'd like to get her out of here before they start on her with that pointed stick."

Reo's eyes rolled around. "You're joshin' me, ain't you?"

"No."

"Then, you're plumb loco. Hell, at least we ought to wait till after midnight. They'll be half drunk and all tired out from dancing by then."

"No," Buchanan said again. "Let's take her out of here now, Johnny."

"Now?" Reo asked, incredulous.

"Right now. You see if you can get our horses ready, and a spare for the girl. I'll drift on down to that wickiup and see if I can slip inside. Most of the tribe's starting to gather down by the ceremonial fire. They've got their horses pegged out behind the knoll back there, and I only spotted two guards. They'll probably mosey on down to the fire once the drums get started. You post yourself in the trees back there until the horse guards leave. I'll bring the girl with me and meet you back there. Have the horses ready. We'll run off the rest of the horses and get the hell out of here."

Reo gave him a look of downright disgust. He said, "Rammin' around in the thick of the Apache stronghold at night. That your idea of usin' your head?"

"If we play it right, we'll have horses. They won't. It ought to give us enough of a jump to stay ahead of them."

"In a pig's eye," Reo said, and spat out the side of his mouth.

Buchanan, his eyes fiercely blue against the dark skin, laid his stare against Reo and said in a very gentle way, "I'm getting a little tired of you fighting me every step of the way, Johnny. It's about time you fish or cut bait."

Reo tried to stare him down; his face was truculent

and almost as red as his hair. Buchanan held his gaze,
level and even. And in time Reo shook his head,
looked away, and said, "Damnit. All right." And swung
up into the brush without any further remarks.

On his way into the camp, Buchanan encountered
old Sentos, who peered out from under his stovepipe
hat with an expression that suggested he was only an
old man with bad kidneys and he wished the world
would let him alone. Grim as a pallbearer, Sentos
pointed his finger in the general direction of Buchanan's
belly button, which would have been the level of an
average man's chest.

"My heart is sad," Sentos said. "You are my good
friend, but the people of the village wish that I do not
ask you to stay any longer here."

"Sure," Buchanan said. "That's all right. I just sent
my partner up to get our horses. We're fixing to pull
out."

"It is wise," Sentos said without pleasure. "I do not
wish that you leave here, not for myself."

"I understand, amigo."

Sentos' lip curled slightly. "I am an old man and I
should not be war chief here. But the best warriors are
no longer with us. They squat fat and slow on the white
man's reservation. And I am here with what is left. I
am chief here only because among crows even a hawk
is an eagle."

"I wish you luck," Buchanan told him.

Sentos shuffled past, toward the gathering crowd at
the ceremonial fire. Long blue lances of twilight shot
across the sky, spreading darker waves across the
mountains.

A tall shape weaved through the shadows, coming
toward Buchanan. It was Matesa, the out-size warrior
who had wanted to kill him back along the trail. Matesa was a little drunk; he smelled of tiswin and horse
sweat. He stood swaying before Buchanan and slapped
his own chest. "To fight Matesa is to die." The big

Indian had a sharp, irritating laugh, like a small dog's yap.

"Well," Buchanan said, "I'm a peaceable man. I've got no fight with you."

"We will fight," Matesa said. He focused his eyes. "Soon," he added, and lurched away toward the ceremonial crowd. A smaller Indian came along, glanced at Buchanan, and rushed after Matesa, following the big warrior, carping like a magpie. Matesa stopped, brought the smaller Indian into focus, roared a single word, and clouted the smaller Indian with one blow that laid him out flat. Matesa looked back at Buchanan, grinned loosely, and went on his way. Down by the fire the shaman was exhorting the spirits, and the crowd was silent. Each of the medicine man's remarks was received as attentively as a ransom note. That was good; as long as the whole tribe's undivided attention was on the proceedings at the fire, Buchanan would be able to prowl the camp unmolested.

Or so he thought. When he reached the girl's wickiup, he found three Indians guarding the door—two bucks and a fat woman.

Buchanan's mouth tightened. He walked right up to the wickiup. The two warriors stiffened and faced him foursquare. The fat woman closed one eye and peered at Buchanan out of the other one.

Buchanan spoke in Apache: "The shaman Lazen wishes that you come to him."

The woman frowned, looked at her two brown companions, and returned her one-eyed stare to Buchanan, who lounged casually and smiled at her.

Finally she spoke sharply to the two braves and waddled away.

Buchanan took out his tobacco and spun up a cigarette. He saw the woman's broad back disappear into the crowd. He turned to the two braves and held out the cigarette, offering it to them. Not speaking, both men shook their heads gravely. Buchanan grinned, put

the cigarette in his mouth, and shifted his stance to get
his fist into the pocket of his Levi's to find a match.

And then, in a blur of motion, he whipped up his
great hands and wrapped them around the two Indians'
thick necks. He brought their skulls together with a
sickening crash. He let them drop, senseless, to the
ground.

Without even troubling to look over his shoulder he
ducked swiftly into the wickiup.

She cringed back against the wall. They had dressed
her in a deerskin dress; her hair was burred; she was
black and blue with bruises, the marks of beatings at
the hands of the squaws. But she was beautiful; no
battering could change that.

Buchanan stared at her until she blushed. She said in
a hoarse voice, "How can you bear to look at me?"

"You look fine," he said gently. "Come on, we're
getting out of here." He took a pace forward and
extended his hand.

She flattened herself against the wall, drawing her
knees up. Buchanan stopped where he was and
crouched over to clear the low ceiling; he said softly,
"They've got you pretty scared, haven't they? Well,
that's all right, then. You'll be all right. There's no
danger now."

Her lips trembled, but she spoke with spunk.
"You're a bad liar."

He smiled. "You're a hard girl to lie to. My name's
Buchanan. Your daddy sent me to get you."

Showing her confusion, she said, "But——"

"No time to talk," he said. "We've got to move. Can
you walk?"

She only stared at him, round-eyed. She said, "Do
you really think we can get away?"

"I think we have to try," he murmured.

She was a strong girl; she got her feet under her and
said in a lower, calmer voice, "I don't think I'm afraid
of you anymore. I'll come."

He reached out and took her hand; he smiled at her with as much confidence as he could scare up and he turned to the door, dropping his free hand to the grip of his six-gun.

Inching the blanket aside, he had a quick look. The two guards were still dead to the world. Down by the fire, half hidden by the jut of Sentos' hut in front of Buchanan, the Apaches squatted around the circle, intent on the shaman's incantations. Colored smoke wafted into the darkening sky. The drums rolled with heady monotony; the singers chanted. A disturbance was starting up around the shape of a fat woman. She was just finding out that the shaman hadn't sent for her after all; she knew, by now, that Buchanan had lied to her to draw her away from the wickiup.

"We've only got a few seconds," he said. "We'll have to run for it."

"I'll keep up," Marinda said.

"On the run, then." He dodged outside, lifting his gun; he waited for her, took her hand again, and ducked around behind the wickiup. No one shouted.

"So far, so good. Keep down. We'll try and keep the wickiup between us and them. Ready?"

"Yes."

"Go!" He gave her a boost, fell into step, and kept stride with her, slowing his pace to match hers. They plunged into the brush and worked their way uphill. Branches scratched the girl's face, and she tore them aside impatiently, never complaining. Her bare, pale feet flitted across the stony ground.

Buchanan risked a quick look over his shoulder. He could see the fat woman jogging toward the wickiup. Just then she lifted her head—and saw him. She stopped, filled her chest, and let out a roar.

"Fat's in the fire," Buchanan grunted. "Come on." He took tight hold on Marinda's arm and half lifted her forward, increasing the pace; they scrambled up the steep pitch, threaded a patch of rocks, and plunged over the top of the rise.

A single gunshot boomed somewhere back in camp; and then they were past the crest, with the ridge between them and the Indians. The girl cried out, lurched, and would have fallen but for Buchanan's tight grip on her arm.

"You hit?"

"No. I must have cut my foot."

Buchanan bent down, got an arm behind her knees and the other around her shoulders, and lifted her bodily. Cradling her in his arms, he ran down the slope toward the Apache horse herd. She didn't seem to weigh any more than a feather.

He could see Johnny Reo emerging from a clump of junipers by the horses; Reo waved his hat. The light was getting rapidly worse. Reo's red hair seemed colorless; the earth had changed from brown-yellow to gray.

The horses were stirring nervously. Buchanan reached the edge of the herd and ran right into the midst of the milling horses; the animals began to scatter, eyes rolling. He slammed right on through. When he was close to Reo, Reo said in a warning voice, "Those two horse guards ain't got far yet. They're battin' around someplace."

Buchanan lifted the girl bodily and set her down astride one of the three saddled horses Reo was holding. Buchanan swung, all part of the same motion, and whipped the reins out of Reo's hand; he handed them up to the girl, who was shaking her head as if to clear it, and said tautly, "Hang on, Marinda. We're just about out of the woods."

"Like hell," Reo said.

Buchanan gathered the reins in smooth synchronization with his quick rise to the saddle. It was an Apache saddle, hardly more than stirruped surcingle and blanket. Reo ran past him and leaped onto the back of his horse—and two squat silhouettes appeared on the western hilltop.

"Horse guards," Reo grunted. His gun whipped up and laid hard echoes across the dusk. The two Indians wheeled to cover. Buchanan reined savagely around and lifted his gun; he fired in the air and whooped, dashing to and fro among the skittish horses. The animals broke and pitched away into the night, scattering in all directions, trailing the dangling ends of the rope hobbles that Reo had cut loose.

Two or three guns opened up, talking in harsh signals from the ridge tops toward Sentos' camp. Buchanan calmed his horse down and lifted his gun. His sights settled on a shifting figure on the ridge, and then he recognized the stovepipe hat. He lowered the gun without firing. He said, "Due north—run for it. Come on."

With the girl between them, they spurred out of the hollow, ramming at a dead run up into the piñons. The ridge behind them blossomed with gunfire. Marinda's hair, silver in the starlight, flowed lawlessly behind her. Laid low across the withers, they drummed onto the ridge, dropped onto the farther slope, and thundered north.

Buchanan urged his horse down the side of the ridge. Flashing into the pines, he led Reo and Marinda recklessly through the timber, humped across a sharp rise of earth, and smashed through brushy undergrowth. Here he held up his arm and paused to breathe the animals. Reo's horse snorted and sneezed.

Buchanan said, "We turn east here."

"East? That's the long way."

"Sure. But it'll take them longer to pick up our trail. We've got to keep zigzagging."

Marinda said, "I have to say something."

Reo turned and stared at her. The girl said, "I want to thank both of you. Even if we don't make it. I have to say it now."

"Don't worry," Buchanan told her. "We're just about home."

They put their horses forward, east, straight away from their previous course; Buchanan held the pace to a steady canter that conserved the horses' wind. Ahead stood the jagged tilts of the broken mountains, tier below tier to the desert flats many miles away. They skirted a thicket; beyond it the grade swung upward in a stiff pitch that put the horses to hard-breathing labor until they achieved the crest and made a long slant downward through open growth. Behind and above them there was the thinned report of a rifle shot—a rallying signal. The echo rolled across the mountains. They ran through a broken district of deep-slashed coulees and cutbanks and gnarled rocks. In the darkness the big bones of Buchanan's face seemed to press more firmly against his skin. *Just about home*— that was what he had said. But it wasn't true. It was a long way home.

Chapter Thirteen

STEVE *Quick sat* in the ranch house parlor, dragging suicidally on a cigarette, pulling from the mouth of a bottle of whisky, and staring sightlessly across the room.

Antonia came in through the front hall. Her big breasts thrust defiantly against her blouse. "Here you are."

"Thinking," he said.

"About what?"

"The old man, in there."

"The old man," Antonia said. "Is he still alive?"

"Yes."

"Why?"

It made him turn his sour glance on her. He groaned. "I'm all shot to shingles, you know that?"

"You've lost your guts," she said contemptuously.

The front door banged open. Race Koenig came in,

deposited his tally book on the desk, and went back
toward the front door. He gave both of them a look
through his eyeglasses and said, "Better turn in, Steve.
Lot of work tomorrow."

"I'll be along."

Koenig nodded. " 'Night, 'Tonia."

When the door closed behind him, Antonia said,
"You want to look out for him. He's twice as tough as
he looks."

"You ought to know," Quick said.

"Stop that. He's never laid a finger on me."

"Sure."

She sighed with mock patience. "Have it your own
way, then. But have you thought about what you'll do
about him afterward?"

"I'll double-cross that bridge when I come to it,"
Quick said, and snickered at his own bad joke.

"You're drunk."

"No. I haven't done much damage to this bottle
yet."

"Put it away," she said. "You've had enough. It's got
to be tonight. Remember? That's what you said."

He snapped, "You've been batting your gums so
much I'm surprised you ain't got bunions on your
lips."

"I'd shut up fast enough if you'd get out of that chair
and go in there after the old man."

"I need a little more whisky first," he said. "It ain't
every day you shoot a cripple dead." He made a bitter
face and turned to stab out the butt of his cigarette in
the pottery ashtray.

He was like that, half-turned in the chair, when he
saw Mike Warrenrode roll into the room in his wheelchair.

Hot anger flashed in Warrenrode's eyes. "So," he
said, biting his words off short, "you aim to kill yourself a cripple, do you?"

Antonia said icily, "You're worth more dead than
alive, you old son of a bitch. And I'm glad you gave

me the chance to say it to your face before you die. I'll bet nobody's ever enjoyed anything as much as I'm going to enjoy watching my own father die."

Warrenrode just sat there for a long stretching moment while the blood drained out of his face and he stared, disbelieving, at Antonia.

Then his face regained its color, and he roared, "You are not, and never have been, any blood kin of mine. Don't ever call me your father. You're a worthless slut, and if it hadn't been for a promise I made your old man before he died, I'd have thrown you out years ago."

"My old man?" she said in a small voice.

"Yes, by God. Your old man was a cowhand that worked for me. A common cowhand, no better, but I liked him. He got stomped by a horse he was trying to break. I promised him I'd look after you as if you were my own daughter."

Antonia's lip curled into a sneer. "And all these years you let me go right on believing I was your bastard daughter."

"You could believe what you wanted to believe. I never said a word to make you think anything of the sort." Warrenrode whipped his leonine head around and fastened his steel glare on Quick. "And you. Of all the lily-livered, backstabbin' cowards I've met in my life, you take top honors. Why don't you go ahead and murder yourself a cripple? Here he is, right in front of you. Or is your chicken-boned hand shaking too badly to hit me at this range?"

Quick was watching the blanket that covered the old man's knees. Under that blanket, he was sure, was the same gun the old man had used to shoot Ben Scarlett. For all Quick could tell, it was pointed right at his heart right now.

And so Quick said in a weak voice, "I don't know what the hell you're talking about."

"You know, I'd have bet my last dollar you'd say that." Warrenrode gave him a look of arch contempt.

"Now I'll tell you what I'm going to do. I'm going to have the two of you stripped naked and tarred and feathered and ridden off this ranch on a rail. And if I ever get wind of either one of you within five hundred miles of here again, I'll turn the dogs loose on you."

Warrenrode turned his face toward the front of the house and dragged in a deep breath. It was clear he intended to yell out. Koenig and the others would come charging in hell-for-leather.

An instant's vision, of all his dreams collapsing like broken glass, flashed through Steve Quick's mind; and it was desperation that sent his hand whipping down to his gun, brought the gun up, and tightened his finger in spasm on the trigger.

Half in awe, half not believing his own act, Quick watched Mike Warrenrode look around at him with vast surprise. For a heart-stopping instant Quick was sure he had missed; he stared, as if mesmerized, and waited for Warrenrode to blast him down in his tracks.

And then Warrenrode slumped forward and fell out of the wheelchair.

The blanket fell away. Warrenrode's spindly legs were tangled up in the chair; it capsized on him.

Quick took four paces and knelt by the old man. He said in a muffled tone, "No gun. He never had no gun under the blanket. The old bastard was bluffing all the time." He cackled harshly like a hen.

"Is he dead?" Antonia asked in a tiny voice.

"See for yourself."

"Tell me. Is he dead?"

He looked up. She was backing away with her hand to her mouth. The table brought her up short and she stood there, face like chalk.

"He's dead," Quick said. He got up, glanced at the front door, and wheeled to the desk. Warrenrode always kept a six-gun in there, a .44-40, same as Quick's gun. Hurriedly Quick yanked the drawer open, took out the gun, and put it into his holster. He put his own gun into the drawer and slammed it shut. Then he stepped away from the desk and said in a taut voice, "When they come in, let me do the talking, and back me up, no matter what I say."

She stammered. "Any—anything you say." She began to chew on her lower lip like a little girl caught in the cookie jar.

Quick said angrily, "Get a goddamn grip on yourself."

He didn't have time to add anything. The door slammed open, and Koenig charged in. Koenig skidded to a stop on his bootheels and looked down with broad wonder at the corpse all tangled up in the overturned wheelchair.

"What——?"

Quick held out both hands, empty. Koenig straightened up, his frown narrowing, and reached slowly toward his gun. Quick snapped his own gun out and said, "Wait a minute. No need to fill the air with bullets, Race. I didn't shoot him."

"Then, who did?"

The crew began to crowd inside. Quick said, "Here, take a look at my gun. You'll see it ain't been fired." He thrust the gun eagerly under Koenig's nose. Koenig took the gun, peered down the barrel, sniffed at it, and opened the loading gate to check the loads. "Sure enough," he said in bewilderment. He gave it back, and Quick dropped it into his holster.

Someone said, "Who did it, Steve?"

Quick took a ragged breath. "It was that Buchanan fellow. The crowd-sized hairpin that was here before, the one Mike sent after Marinda."

Koenig said, "Buchanan? What would he shoot Mike for?"

"I dunno," Quick said. "I only heard a snatch of it. Buchanan must've sneaked inside the back way. When I came in, him and the old man were arguing hot and heavy. Buchanan was sayin' the Apaches had killed Marinda, but he wanted his money anyway, the money the old man promised him if he brought Marinda back

alive. The old man refused to pay him. Said Buchanan
hadn't delivered and didn't have no gold coming.
Buchanan said he'd taken a big risk on Mike's account
and he figured that was worth some money. It got
pretty hot and heavy, like I said. Buchanan finally
dragged out his gun and shot the old man. I came in
with 'Tonia, there. We was just in time to see Buchanan
duckin' out through the back hallway, there."

Koenig cursed. "By now he's a mile away."

Quick risked a sidewise glance at Antonia. She had
regained her composure; she was looking at him as if
she were pleasantly surprised, as if she were proud of
his ingenuity.

One of the hands headed for the door. "I dunno
about the rest of you gents, but I'm going to slap a
saddle on a bronc and see if I can't pick up the
bastard's trail."

"Yeah," another man said.

"Damn right. Come on, Pete."

The crew filed out quickly. Koenig's voice reached
after them. "A couple of you stick around. Somebody's
got to tend to Mike's body and keep Antonia company."

Quick said, "Antonia's the boss now, Race."

"What?"

"Sure. With Marinda dead and the old man dead,
Antonia's the only blood relative left to claim the Pitchfork."

Koenig's puzzled frown shifted to the girl. "I never
heard nothing about you being Mike's kin."

"It's true," she said. She was making a good act of
being grief-stricken.

Quick said calmly, "You calling the lady a liar,
Race?"

"I'll have to have more than your word on it,"
Koenig said stubbornly.

"Sure, easy enough," Quick said. "Check with that
lawyer in town, Ford. He'll testify for 'Tonia."

"I don't know," Koenig said, scratching his jaw.

Quick laughed and said placatingly, "It'll all work out, Race. You'll see. You and me, we'll make peace between us."

"You're asking a lot of a good hater."

"We're friends, Race. Remember?"

"Maybe," Koenig said. "But the next time you pull a gun on me, one of us will be a dead friend." With that he swung with a snap of his wide shoulders. "We'll talk it out later. Right now I'm going after Buchanan."

"I'll stick around here and keep an eye on things," Quick said.

When Koenig left, Quick turned his enigmatic glance toward Antonia. She came up to him and hooked her arm in his. She said, "I can be *very* affectionate if you know how to treat me, Steve. And I think you're learning how to treat me." She smiled up into his face.

Chapter Fourteen

IT must have been around two in the morning. There was no moon, but Buchanan's eyes were used to the darkness by now; he had no trouble picking up the movement of six or eight horsemen filing quickly over the pass a mile ahead of him. The horsemen had to cross an open flat of pale rock shale, and that was what gave them away.

Buchanan reined in. Marinda halted beside him; and Johnny Reo, who had been riding rear guard, caught up and said cheerlessly, "Didn't take them long to round up them horses. How in hell'd they get out ahead of us?"

"They know the country better than we do," Buchanan said. "No sense crying about it. At least they haven't spotted us yet."

"Yet."

Marinda said, "What will we do now?"

"One thing for sure," Buchanan said. "We can't ride through that pass up there. We'll have to cut north or south."

"They'll expect us to go north," Reo said. "I vote we head south, try to lose ourselves in the timber. Nothing up north of here but rock mesas and the most God-awful desert you ever saw."

Buchanan considered it. He offered his canteen to Marinda, who drank gratefully; he said presently, "No. They'll figure we're too smart to head north, so they're more likely to look for us in the trees south of here. That wasn't any accident, those six Apaches riding big as life through that pass up yonder. They wanted us to see them. They want us to turn south. If we go south, we get farther from home every step we go."

"So?" Reo said.

"So we go north," Buchanan said, and put his horse that way.

They rammed through the mountains at a steady gait, sparing the horses but eating up ground. It was an hour or more of hard riding, without talk, until finally the girl pulled her horse close by Buchanan's and reached out weakly to pluck his sleeve.

"I'm dizzy, I can't breathe. I'm sorry—can we stop for a little while?"

Buchanan drew rein. "Sure," he said. "Horses need a rest anyhow."

When Reo opened his mouth to object, Buchanan shook his head mutely and gave Reo a pointed look. Reo subsided. They dismounted in a foothill boulder field, watered the horses sparingly from their hats, and sat down with rifles across their laps. "Ten or fifteen minutes," Buchanan said. "It's all we can spare."

"Come daylight," Reo admonished, "they'll pick up our tracks. We want to be long gone by then."

"You want to put wings on these horses, Johnny? You go right ahead."

Reo grumbled something and tugged off one boot to scratch the sole of his foot. "Been itching for two hours now," he said.

Buchanan said, "Shake out that boot before you put it back on. No telling what might crawl into it." He gave Reo a deadpan glance.

Marinda said, "Someone told me once that Indians wouldn't fight at night."

"Somebody told me that, too," Buchanan said. "But I reckon nobody told the Indians."

Reo's lip twisted. "You want to say something else funny?"

"Simmer down, Johnny. You're not mad at me. You're mad because for once in your life you got scared."

Reo thought about that. "Maybe you're right." He shook out his boot and yanked it on. "But you got to admit, a thing like this can ruin your whole day."

Marinda said, "Do you think they're following us right now?"

"Not following," Reo said. "Chasing." He got to his feet and started away. "I'd better go on up top for a look-see down the back trail."

Buchanan watched him go. Reo tended to complain a lot, but he had just as much courage as the next man. His constant beefing, you learned after a while, was only a mannerism. Buchanan hadn't forgotten the calm deliberation with which Reo had outdrawn Cesar Diaz, or the sizzling accuracy of Reo's rifle marksmanship on that first day when Reo had pitched in against the Warrenrode crew. Buchanan thought of Lance Corporal Ivy, the truculent soldier. It seemed a hell of a long time ago; actually it wasn't more than a few days.

This country was full of luck. Some found it, some didn't. So far, Buchanan's luck was holding. He was still alive.

Sometimes he felt as though he were at war with the inevitable. It was a curious thing how a peaceable man could find himself dead center in a mountain of troubles.

His glance eased around toward the girl. She was leaning back against a rock, eyes almost closed. She'd been through a meat grinder, that was for sure. Abused and bruised by the Apache women, she couldn't be blamed for exhaustion. He hadn't yet heard her utter a single whimper.

One thing was sure. She was an orchid in a cactus garden. She was a willowy beauty; her eyes could melt a man down into a puddle.

She seemed to feel his attention. She lifted her eyelids and looked at him. "Tell me something."

"What's that?"

"Do you honestly think we have a chance?"

"I reckon," Buchanan said.

"I'm glad you said that, even if it's a lie." She stirred, pressing both hands to her temples and brushing her hair back with her palms. She said, "Your partner—he's only here for the money my father offered him. That's true, isn't it?"

"You'd have to ask Johnny about that."

"But it wasn't the money that made you come."

"What makes you think so?" he asked.

"It's one of those things a woman can tell. I can't explain it any better than that."

"Lady," he said, "no matter what happens, it's been worth it to meet you." He grinned at her.

She said softly, "Lady? Buchanan, I can tell you this—scratch a lady, and you'll find a woman."

He considered her gravely after that, but he had no time to compose an answer. The soft scuff of leather on gravel sent him spinning around, palming his gun.

"Easy," Johnny Reo hissed, and appeared vaguely in the night.

Buchanan said, "I'd better hang a bell on you so I'll know where you are. I told you once before to make more noise when you come up behind me."

Reo walked in, and as soon as Buchanan saw his face, he knew something was wrong.

Reo said, "Just pretend like you're General Custer and old Sentos is Sitting Bull. We got some company comin' up behind us."

"How far back?"

"Twenty minutes, maybe. No more."

Buchanan strode across the ground to catch up the horses. "Let's go, then."

Daylight whiplashed his eyes. The morning sun blazed unforgivingly, pouring rivulets of sweat down Buchanan's body under the thin shirt. The white glare sent fragments of light against his eyes like painful metal slivers.

On laboring horses they lined out across the flats, leaving the foothills behind. Wherever the Apaches were, they hadn't put in an appearance.

They passed a goat-herding family of Papago Indians, whereupon Reo gave Buchanan a disgusted look; there was no doubt the Papagos would give the Apaches an exact description of the three white riders and the direction they were riding.

But there was nothing to do about that. They prowled forward into the desert, toward a monumental rock spire that measured a good half mile across at its base. It towered several hundred feet in the air; its top was cut off, flat as a table.

Buchanan twisted in the saddle to look back—and found half a dozen horsemen driving forward at a gallop, raising a good deal of dust. There was no mistaking the determined flatness of their run, nor the fact that they were aiming right for Buchanan and his companions.

Plunging spurs into the horses' flanks, Reo and Buchanan laid themselves low in the saddles and whooped the girl forward, swinging in an arc to bypass the end of the tall mesa. To escape being trapped

against the monument, they would have to beat the
advancing riders to the end of the mesa, then get
around and beyond it before the Apaches came within
rifle range.

They might have done it, too, on fresh horses. The
game ponies settled evenly into the low, leg-stretching
smoothness of the thundering dead run; but the speed
of freshness wasn't there. Stones and dust flew up behind the drumming hoofs. The ground was uneven,
pitted with angry scars and holes. An ocotillo raked
Buchanan's arm, tearing the sleeve away, leaving
streaks on his skin like a cat's claws.

They had to slow the gait to pound through a patch
of saddle-sized rocks; and when they cleared it, with
four hundred yards yet to run, Buchanan whipped a
glance over his shoulder.

The six riders had fanned out wide. They charged
down in earnest, close enough for him to see their
band-tied hair and rifles lifted at arm's length. They
didn't waste any breath whooping or shouting. They
were running on a tangent with the line of the fugitives'
course, only a quarter-mile away.

Johnny Reo's curses fell against the laid-back ears of
his horse. They swept toward the bend in the cliff, and
the nearest Indian's rifle opened up.

Buchanan did not hear the strike of the bullet any-
where nearby. The sun-battered country glittered, and
the horses' metal shoes made a hard racket over the
rocky earth. A foam of sweat burst out on Buchanan's
horse. Rifles cranged behind him; two or three bullets
screamed off the cliff, one of them close enough for
Buchanan to see the white strip it tore out of the rock.
That was uncommon shooting at long distance free-
hand. When he glanced back, he saw why it was so
good. Two of the Indians had halted to take aim. They
were too far back to make their shots effective; most of
them fell short. But the other four Apaches kept gain-
ing steadily—the angle of their approach made their
run shorter than the fugitives'.

They were within three hundred yards when Buchanan leaned to the left and swept around the sharp cliff edge, herding Marinda and Reo ahead of him. The Indians massed their fire as he made the turn; he was the target of a vicious fusillade before the horse carried him out of their view behind the jut of the cliff.

The slope on the backside was broken here and there by loose talus slides; they had to run out around them to avoid fouling the horses' feet. All of it glared painfully in the hot sun. Marinda's horse seemed to be lagging; and a glance that way made Buchanan's jaw clamp tight. The horse was bleeding from a bullet slice across the flank. It was not a serious wound, but it would defeat them in any cross-country chase.

He looked back. It wouldn't be more than a few seconds before the Apaches would whip into sight.

Buchanan yelled at Reo, got his attention, and held up his arm. Reo's face instantly creased into a frown, and he said, "No, goddamn it. What the hell for?" His voice carried over the thunder of hoofbeats. But Buchanan shouted at him and guided his running horse in close to the toe of a sprawled shale slide. Before the horse could stop, Buchanan leaped from the saddle. He wheeled toward Marinda, lifted her bodily off her horse and placed her on his own.

"Work your way up the slope, both of you. Find some cover. Try to find some rocks that don't look too much like tombstones."

Marinda said, "But what about you?"

"Just get going," he shouted.

Reo held still long enough to say, "Hope we ain't got our powder wet, amigo."

"Keep close to her."

"Yeah. Well, console yourself with this, amigo—the closer they come, the harder they are to miss."

"Get out of here," Buchanan roared.

Reo went ramming after the girl. Buchanan jogged the rifle in the circle of his fist, slapped the girl's injured horse, and watched it hump away from the mesa. With

a little luck, the horse's dust cloud would conceal the
fact that it didn't have a rider. It might draw the
Apaches in pursuit.

Buchanan scrambled behind the hump of the talus
slide, dropping flat on painfully sharp rock slivers just
as four Apaches raced into sight.

He jacked a shell into the chamber and braced the
rifle against his cheek.

One of the Apaches wheeled after the riderless horse;
but the others came ramming close along the base of
the cliff, straight toward Buchanan.

He squinted against the glare and squeezed off a
shot. Without waiting to see its effect, he swung to bear
on a second rider and his steady pressure on the trigger
made the gun go off. It caught him almost by surprise.

The first Indian pitched from his horse and rolled to
a limp hunched stop. The second threw up his arms but
kept his seat, lurching in the saddle. Buchanan took
unhurried aim and dropped that man with a shot that
recoiled heavily against his shoulder.

Reo's rifle was banging away from the rocks some
distance upslope. He was concentrating his fire on the
lone Indian who had gone after the riderless horse.
That one was almost out of range when one of Reo's
bullets knocked him off his horse.

Buchanan got to one knee, lifting the rifle with him.
One Indian was circling, out of range, and it was about
time for those other two to come running past the end
of the cliff.

They didn't.

Buchanan nodded. He reloaded the rifle and turned,
starting to make his way up toward the rocks where
Reo and the girl had taken cover—and a bullet
smashed into the talus, making a racket like a pebble
crashing around inside a metal drum. It drove
Buchanan to cover, flat against the ground. His mind
automatically analyzed the high, flat report of the rifle.
*Long-range stuff. Maybe a .38-56, a small slug backed
by a lot of gunpowder.*

He inched his head up to spot the rifleman's position. There wasn't any more shooting. That lone Indian out on the flats was circling beyond rifle range; it was hard to tell what he had in mind. Buchanan felt the dryness of his lips and wished he had his canteen. The sun was a brass fist that slugged the back of his shirt.

A bullet whined off the rocks. *Just to let us know he's still there*, Buchanan thought.

A new thought grenaded into his mind: it was stalemate right now, but if the Indians kept them pinned here very long, Sentos' reinforcements would come up.

Echoing that thought, Johnny Reo's call came echoing down the slope: "We got to get out of here, Buchanan."

Buchanan gave the desert a regretful look; and finally he tossed his head back and answered Reo. "You two go on. I'll try to hold them up here."

Faintly he could hear the girl's immediate protest. Reo argued with her. Buchanan couldn't make out the words, but he had already thought of all the arguments. There were three of them and only two horses; there was a chance for two to escape but not for all three. There were a dozen arguments. They all came back to the same thing. Two horses, three riders. Those Indian ponies were too far away to catch.

Reo's voice rocketed down: "All right, amigo. Give us some cover if you can.".

"I'll see you on the Pitchfork," Buchanan answered. "Good luck."

"Yeah. So long, you big bastard!"

Marinda's voice came down, less loud but just as strong. "*Vaya con Dios*, Buchanan."

"Here we go!" Reo roared.

Buchanan didn't watch them. He kept his attention on the end of the cliff. He heard the two horses go clattering down toward the desert. When a rifle started talking down at the end of the cliff, Buchanan opened up with a savage fire, blasting into the Indian's telltale puff of gunsmoke, raking the rocks with a fury of

bullets. It shut the Indian off. Buchanan levered and
fired, levered and fired. When his ammunition ran dry,
he yanked out his pistol and emptied that as well.

Quickly thumbing cartridges into his guns, he
snapped a glance across the desert. Reo and Marinda
were well out on the flats, riding hell for leather. The
lone Indian out there was galloping toward them. Reo's
horse sat back on its haunches, throwing a spume of
dust forward; Reo's gun barked three or four times,
and the Indian slumped on his horse. Then Reo and
the girl went on.

Guns were blasting in harsh signals again, but Reo
and Marinda were beyond bullet range. Buchanan
drove another bullet into the rocks down there. There
were at least two Apaches there, if more hadn't come
up.

Then the silence settled down. The close heat made
his skin crawl with sweat. The metal lockplate of the
rifle began to sear his palm. Time slowed, and he felt as
lonely as he'd ever been. Out on the flats a buzzard
circled low over the dead Indians. Thirst built up in
Buchanan's throat, and to keep the saliva going he
popped a pebble in his mouth and worked it around
with his tongue. Coated with dirt and sweat, he lay in
the direct rays of the desert sun. His lids were gritty;
his eyes turned raw. He watched the buzzard's slow,
evasive descent. Four other birds joined it in the air.
Gradually they settled on one of the dead men, fighting
among themselves for the prime delicacy, the eyes.
There was a beating of black wings and a brief,
squawking dispute. One of the buzzards flapped over to
the nearby corpse. Their ugly necks bent down.

A rifle shot splashed against the talus slide.
Buchanan leaned back, resigned and fatalistic. The shot
startled the buzzards into the air, but they settled down
again slowly to their meal.

Buchanan's ears picked up the faint thudding of
hoofbeats, moving at a trot. They faded quickly, leaving silence.

It could mean any number of things. There was only one way to find out for sure. Buchanan put his hat on his rifle and lifted it slowly in the air. When that drew no fire, he pulled the hat down and put it on, and stood up slowly, rifle ready.

Nothing stirred. Buchanan took a firmer grip on the rifle and stepped boldly into the open.

No reaction. Well, then, maybe they'd decided to surprise him by circling around the other side of the mesa. That would take them a little time. Time enough, maybe, for Buchanan to get out onto the flats far enough to hold them at bay with his rifle. It was for certain he'd have a better chance out there than trapped here in the rocks. He'd be moving all the time toward safety—maybe twenty miles of desert to cross before he hit the Pitchfork line, but a man could do that. He was one rifleman against God-knew-how-many Indians, but out on the open desert they'd make fine targets if they came within range. And it wasn't for nothing that it had been said of Tom Buchanan, *You can tell what Buchanan aims at by what he hits.*

Anyhow, it was the best gamble he had. Anything was better than roasting immobile in these bake-oven rocks. At least there was freedom in being in motion, and to Buchanan that kind of freedom was the sweetest taste of all.

He started walking briskly toward the northwest, toward Pitchfork.

The buzzards circled resentfully into the air as his path brought him close to them. They hovered only a few feet overhead, wings beating, unblinking. When he passed, they descended to finish. He didn't glance at the dead Indians. He didn't want to see their vacant eye sockets and torn flesh. His boots stirred little whorls of dust; his spurs dragged the ground.

He covered a hundred yards, then two hundred; and a gunshot cracked across the desert.

He wheeled, searching, bringing up the rifle. A shot came again; he felt it fan by his cheek. He saw the little puff of rising smoke at the far end of the great rock monument.

He dropped belly-flat to make a smaller target and laid his cheek along the hot rifle stock. An Indian rode out into the open, maybe four hundred yards from where Buchanan lay; and a second Indian's rifle fired steadily from the rocks, beating up the dust, making spouts and creases in the earth all around Buchanan.

The nearest cover was a clump of catclaw fifty feet away, not big enough to conceal a gopher. But he had to act. You couldn't just lie there and wait for a chance bullet to finish you.

A bullet thumped into the earth near enough to shake it. Buchanan flinched.

The horseback Indian shook his fisted rifle overhead and kneed his horse forward at a canter. Across the silent air Buchanan faintly heard his whoops.

The Apache was attacking to count coup for his fallen comrades.

Buchanan breeched a shell and laid his eyes to the sights, holding his breath back in his chest. The Apache was firing as he rode, but there was only chance danger from those one-handed shots; and now the Indian was in his companion's line-of-fire, and there was no more shooting from the rocks.

Buchanan's finger curled around the trigger, and he felt the pound of his heart in his chest. He lay sprawled in the open, every minute a better target for the charging rider. The Apache was laid flat down on his horse with only one leg and arm showing—good horsemanship for an Apache. His one-handed shooting was even more erratic as he took cover with his face half-buried in the withers. Buchanan lowered his eye to the rear tang sight. If he didn't get a better shot soon, he would have to down the horse and shoot the Indian falling free—if the Indian didn't drop behind the horse for cover.

He recognized the Apache then by his size. It was the

brute Matesa. *We will fight soon,* Matesa had said. *To fight Matesa is to die.*

That was why Matesa was coming at him in the open. It was a personal thing, man to man.

It was then, ready to fire, when Buchanan felt a hot, stinging flash in the face and found himself instantly blinded. Reaction closed his hand; the rifle went off, charging his shoulder.

One of Matesa's wild bullets had spewed sand in his eyes.

Buchanan clawed at his face. The grit was like fire in his eyes, and he could see nothing but a blood-red haze. He heard the ram of hoofs and Matesa's excited cry of triumph, the slam of the rifle, the slap of the bullet into the ground near enough to spray his cheek.

Buchanan rolled over violently, blinking, feeling the tears wet his cheeks. His pulse pounded louder than the on-rushing hoofs. He scraped fingers across his eyes, hazy vision returned slowly to his right eye. He held it open long enough to see painfully through the cloud.

Matesa was almost on top of him.

There was no time to aim. Buchanan rammed the buttstock against the ground, barrel pointing upward, and pulled trigger with one hand, his other hand shoving the ground to roll him aside from the trampling, pointed hoofs.

His rifle roared. Buchanan rolled over on his back, blinking fast. He saw the horse rush past a foot away, a gray blur of movement; he saw the slug drive Matesa back, punching a great hole in his face, and saw Matesa's head rock back, the rifle flying from dead fingers to skitter across the desert.

Matesa fell off the back of the running horse with a crunch of sound and slid along the ground. He came to rest in an awkward, crushed position.

Buchanan rubbed his eyes, squinted, blinked, and made faces. The horse wheeled wearily and came to a stand, as it must have been trained to do.

Back in the rocks the last Apache's rifle opened up

in a fury. Buchanan dug sand out of his eyes, uttered a curse, and fired not very accurately at the rocks. It shut the Indian up for a moment. Buchanan sprinted toward the standing horse. It dodged away from him suspiciously. He spoke soothing words and got a flying grip on the single trailing rein. The horse almost yanked it out of his fist. He still couldn't see as well as he would have wanted. He hauled the horse's head down and clambered asaddle. The Indian in the rocks started shooting again. Buchanan wheeled the Indian pony around, laid himself low, and spurred it to a gallop. Within half a minute he was beyond the effect of the Apache's distant rifle.

He rode past the Indian Johnny Reo had shot and glanced down as he whipped by. Shock registered on Buchanan's face. The dead warrior was Cuchillo, Sentos' only remaining son. When Sentos discovered that, he'd tear all Arizona apart to find Buchanan and Reo.

Buchanan glanced back. Gunshot echoes carried a long way across this kind of country, and he half expected to see the huge dust cloud of an advancing war party back toward the hills from which he had come during the night. But Sentos and the main bunch had probably guessed Buchanan would go south during the night. It would take a little while for the Apaches to come north.

A little while; not very long. That lone Indian back there was already making dust, back toward the hills to round up Sentos and the others.

Buchanan turned forward and gigged the horse up. Red-eyed and saddle-weary, he rode toward Pitchfork under the blazing sun, and thought vaguely of the dreams of peaceful fishing that had brought him into this country only a few days ago. Somehow it all seemed a little unfair. A man couldn't even find a little peace and quiet.

A rider was galloping toward him from up ahead. Buchanan kept up his pace, but brought his rifle around. His eyes were still not altogether clear; it was some time before he recognized the horseman.

It was Johnny Reo. Reo rode up with a broad grin of relief. He lied cheerfully, "I knew you wouldn't have no trouble at all. Hell, there wasn't more than six Indians to fight."

"Where's Marinda?"

"I left her up ahead. Figured I'd better come back and see if you needed burying or anything."

Reo's irreverent grin was a white slash across his weather-burned face. He swept off his hat to wipe his face in the crook of his sleeve. The bright red hair stood up like a defiant guidon.

Buchanan said, "I told you a long time ago you were a better man than you gave yourself credit for."

"Naw," said Reo. "I only came back to see if you'd left any Indians for me to kill."

They rode north together. Inside fifteen minutes they picked up Marinda along the trail; she fell in with them, showing Buchanan her happy smile. Her nose wrinkled when she laughed; it was clear how glad she was to see him alive.

In an hour they were still south of the Pitchfork boundary, but a crowd of Pitchfork riders were drumming toward them. Johnny Reo grinned. "Sizable welcoming committee there. Can't say I ain't glad to see them, either."

"They may not be too glad to see us once they find out what's after us," Buchanan observed. He had no idea how accurate the first half of his statement was; but he found out soon enough.

Throwing up a stinging pall of dust, the Pitchfork crew skidded to a halt, milling around the three riders. There was a lot of calling back and forth. Race Koenig jumped off his horse, lifted Marinda down in his arms, and held her close to him, crooning to her in a voice that mixed disbelief with joy. Buchanan watched them and thought that the bespectacled foreman was one very lucky man indeed. *In fact,* Buchanan thought . . .

He didn't have time to finish the thought. Half a dozen men ringed him, and he suddenly realized they all had their guns drawn.

"*Now* what?" he said to himself. He spoke to the nearest man in an amiable voice: "Say, now, friend, what's the gun for?"

"Sit back and breathe through your nose, pilgrim," the cowhand snarled.

"Now, wait a minute," Buchanan said. "I can take a joke as well as the next man, but right now I'm kind of tired and beat up and I don't know as I——"

"Shut up," the cowhand snapped.

Race Koenig looked up from his embrace with the girl. He placed her gently to one side and spoke in a flat voice; his eyes had gone cold and hard.

"Bringing Marinda back won't buy you a pardon, Buchanan. If I had my way, I'd chip you down an inch at a time, but the boys decided we'd better turn you over to the law. You're gonna get your neck stretched nice and legal."

Johnny Reo snapped at a rider drifting around, "Can't you hold that damn horse still?" Reo turned his angry attention to Koenig. "What's this all about, mister?"

"Your friend here shot Mike Warrenrode dead last night," said Koenig.

Buchanan felt the cold pressure of a gun in his ribs.

Chapter Fifteen

"*MOVE a muscle*," breathed the rider behind Buchanan, "and you'll never see tomorrow."

Marinda stared at Race Koenig. "My father——?"

"I'm sorry, honey," Koenig said. He wrapped one

arm around her. "You've been through enough, God knows, without this."

"But . . ." she said; she cleared her throat and started again. "But you said Buchanan shot him."

"That's right. He did."

"Last night? At the ranch?"

Koenig nodded. His bleak eyes peered through the dusty glasses at Buchanan, who sat at ease in his saddle with the attitude of a man who had just felt the weight of the last straw that was about to break his back.

Marinda said, "It wasn't Buchanan who did it, Race. I've been with him every minute of the time since yesterday afternoon, and we haven't been within forty miles of the Pitchfork."

She said it in a strong, clear voice, and nobody missed hearing her.

Johnny Reo said, "I'll second what the lady said. We had our hands pretty full last night, and it's for damn sure Buchanan wasn't anyplace around here."

Race Koenig took off his hat and scratched his head. Buchanan felt the gun muzzle recede from his back. He reached around and rubbed the place where the steel had pushed him. His glance was angry, tired, impatient, and intolerant; he said to Koenig, "A man could get in a pack of trouble jumping to confusions the way you do. If I wasn't a mite tired, I might think about cracking a few teeth among the congregation hereabouts."

Koenig was still scratching his head, mostly in embarrassment. "I reckon we made a mistake."

"I reckon you did," Johnny Reo said.

"I reckon we kind of owe you an apology, Buchanan."

Buchanan said, "I'd settle for two shots of whisky, a good meal, and twenty-four hours sleep. But I'll have to take a rain check on the sleep. We're likely to have some Indians for supper."

All in a tight-riding bunch they swept into the Pitchfork yard and dismounted. Steve Quick, in the ranch house door, stiffened when he recognized Buchanan. "You're not dead."

"If I am," Buchanan said, "somebody forgot to bury me."

Koenig stepped past him and walked up to Quick, who backed up against the wall, his eyes growing wide. Koenig said grimly, "I'll just take your gun, Steve."

"What the hell for?"

"I ain't just exactly sure," Koenig said. "But it's for certain you lied out of both sides of your mouth last night. Buchanan didn't kill the old man. Wasn't within forty miles of this place last night."

Steve Quick summoned his bravado. "Just who the hell says he wasn't?"

"I do." Marinda stepped quietly forward out of the crowd.

Quick hadn't even seen her before; she'd been concealed by the crowd and the cloud of dust. Quick's face went three shades paler, and he seemed about to faint.

Antonia appeared in the doorway. She just stood there and stared at Marinda and Buchanan as if she didn't really believe they were alive.

Race Koenig plucked Quick's gun from its holster and stepped back. Quick seemed dazed; he didn't even appear to realize that Koenig had taken his gun away. Quick began to clear his throat in spasms.

Koenig said, "Couple of you boys take him inside and tie him up. Something damned funny going on around here, and we'll have to be gettin' to the bottom of it. But we haven't got time for that right now. Boat, skinny over to the bunkhouse and grab up every gun and cartridge you can find. We'll hole ourselves up in the ranch house. Old Mike built it like a fort against Indians, and I reckon it'll still serve the purpose."

Buchanan said, "Sentos isn't after you or your crew. He's after us, Johnny and me. Give us a brace of fresh horses."

"What for?"

"To outrun those Indians," Buchanan said, "and maybe draw them off you while we're at it."

Reo gave him a disgusted look but kept his mouth shut. Marinda said flatly, "No. Don't let them do it, Race."

" 'Course I won't," Koenig said. "Buchanan, I don't know how you got Marinda away and I don't expect I ever will know all of it. But whatever you did, it took more guts than I've ever seen or heard of. If Mike Warrenrode was alive, he'd back you with every gun he had, and I can't do no different. Pitchfork stands by its own. You two have got protection whether you want it or not."

"I for one," remarked Johnny Reo, "don't aim to argue about that. Buchanan, if you wasn't such a goddamn stupid hero, you'd know when to quit taking chances."

Buchanan said, "Johnny, I can't ask any other man alive to do my fighting for me and I don't think you can either if you stop a minute and think about it."

"I do my own fightin'," Reo said hotly, "which you know damn well."

There was a strange little sound that came out of Antonia's throat. Everyone looked at her. She was standing on the top step, a foot or two above the others, and she was looking out past the yard. Her mouth was open.

A cowboy at the back of the crowd called out, "Dust cloud down there. Thirty or forty horses, maybe."

Reo said to Buchanan, "You see? Ain't no time to make a run for it anyway, you big stupid bastard." He grinned and strode into the house.

It broke the others loose; suddenly there was a fast shifting and milling of men rushing off to gather supplies. They poured into the ranch house and moved swiftly from room to room, battening the heavy siege shutters, laying out rifles by the decade-old gunports. Race Koenig stood by the front door until the last man was inside; he slammed the heavy door and bolted it.

"We've held off bigger gangs than this one," he said, and gave Marinda a false grin and a squeeze of the hand.

They could hear the faint roar of Indian voices, rising to high-pitched war whoops. Buchanan moved to a window and peered out through the small rifle port. He'd had enough Indian fighting to last him the rest of his life, he figured, but there wasn't anything for it but to fight this through to the finish. He had no hatred for those Apaches out there; he wished they would turn around and go in peace.

He saw them, some distance away, leaving their horses and flitting forward on foot. These were Apaches, not Plains Indians, and there was no riding around in circles or breast-beating. Apaches were clever fighters and had a healthy respect for the value of their own skins. They would belly forward to the outbuildings of the ranch and filter from cover to cover. There wouldn't be any easy targets. It promised to be a long siege.

Koenig came by Buchanan's post and said, "We've got plenty of food, and the well's in the center patio where we can get to it. We can outlast them—all summer if we have to. And if I know them, they'll quit after a while."

"And take every head of stock you own with them," Buchanan said.

"Can't be helped."

"It can if we take the fight to them."

"What do you mean?"

"I'll have to work it out," Buchanan said, and squinted upward through the gunport. "Maybe three hours left to sundown. We can't make any moves until after dark." He poked his rifle though the port and fired at the distant shape of a dodging Indian. It was the first shot of the battle. The Indian ducked for cover; and guns began booming all around the fortified adobe house.

It wasn't long before the house stank with the acrid fumes of powdersmoke.

Steve Quick sat in a corner of an empty bedroom, hands tied and feet tied. He was brooding over his misfortunes when Johnny Reo turned into the room, gave him a single, desultory glance, and went to the window. Reo stood there awhile, then lifted his rifle and fired through the slot.

"Missed the bastard," Reo said without heat. He glanced at Quick.

Quick said petulantly, "Quit looking at me like I'm some special kind of bug."

"You've got a lively imagination," Reo said. "I was only thinking you must've been pretty stupid to blame that killing on Buchanan."

"How was I to know you'd get back alive?"

"I reckon you don't know me and Buchanan very well."

"Maybe not," Quick conceded. "How good a gun is Buchanan, anyway?"

"Good enough, I reckon. You can't get deader than dead."

"What about you? That's a fancy gun you're scratching those matches on."

Reo held the flame to his cigarette and shook out the match. His smile was a steel bar. "I got a way with a gun," he admitted.

A light of calculation burned in Steve Quick's eyes. He said slowly, "I hope you don't believe everything Race Koenig tells you about me."

"Amigo," said Reo, "I got a habit. I don't believe everything *any*body tells me."

Something was running through Steve Quick's mind —something Trask had said to him a few days ago. *Reo? He'd set fire to his own mother if he could get a good price for the ashes.*

Reo's rifle snaked up to the window; he squinted and squeezed. The rifle boomed and recoiled. Reo hauled it

down with a grunt of satisfaction and shook his head.
"What mortals these fools be," he muttered, and
chuckled.

"You hit one of them?"

"Uh-huh."

Quick studied him over a stretching period. Finally
he said tentatively, "Maybe you and me could strike up
a bargain, Reo."

It made Reo look at him. "Why should I bargain
with you when I got a corner on the market? You ain't
in no position to make deals. You got nothing left to
bargain with."

"That's where you're wrong," Quick said. "Mosey on
over here where I don't have to shout."

Reo glanced out through the gunport, fired once, and
looked back at Quick. With a shrug and a loose grin,
he came over and hunkered down by Quick. "I'm
listenin'. Better say it right the first time, though, because you may never get another."

Antonia moved through the sulphur-smoky parlor
handing out fresh ammunition. Men were coughing in
the blue haze. Concussion from all the gunfire had
blown out all the lamps, and the room was in half
darkness, with all its shutters closed and the only light
filtering in through the slitted rifle ports. Rays of light
sliced through the smoke.

She gave Buchanan a handful of cartridges. "Kill
some for me," she told him.

His red-shot eyes shifted toward her briefly. She
admired the jut of his big jaw, the man-sized heft of
him, the go-to-hell smile that never seemed very far
from the surface.

But all he said to her was, "If you can find Koenig in
this steambath, ask him to drift over here when he gets
a minute."

She moistened her lips and smiled, but it was wasted;
he was aiming down his sights through the port again.
She pouted and moved on.

She found Marinda stripping away a cowboy's sleeve to wash and bandage a bullet wound. Marinda looked up, without particular expression, and pushed hair out of her eyes. Antonia's eyes flashed. She jerked her head in a gesture and waited for Marinda to come over to her.

Marinda stood up. "What is it?"

"I just want you to think about this," Antonia hissed. "If you think you've got everything you wanted, you're wrong."

"Why, what do you mean?"

"You'll see," Antonia said angrily, and wheeled away into the smoke.

She stopped by Race Koenig and said, "Buchanan wants to talk to you," and went on, distributing the last of the cartridges. That brought her near the hall door. She glanced around to see if anyone was watching; she hiked up her skirts and ran quickly down the hall.

When she pushed the door open, she found Johnny Reo sitting on the floor near her husband.

Quick looked up and grinned. "Hi, honey. Looks like we got some help."

"I was coming to cut you loose," she said.

"Shut the door, then."

Reo uncoiled his lanky frame and went over to the window. He peered through the slot for a bit, didn't seem to see anything to shoot at, and turned back.

Quick said, "A quarter-interest, Reo. One-fourth of the whole shebang. All it takes is three bullets. Koenig, Marinda, and Buchanan if he gets in the way."

Reo said, "Buchanan's sort of a friend of mine."

"Scared of him?" Quick sneered.

"No, I ain't scared of him," Reo said.

"Funny. I had you sized up as a man who measured his loyalties in dollars and cents. A sensible man. One-fourth of the Pitchfork, Reo. Think about it."

"I'm also thinkin' about how far I can trust you to pay off on your promise," Reo said. "And so I'll say this. I'll be sticking to you like a burr until I get paid

off in cash, and it won't bother me much to shoot you
to pieces if you don't come across."

"Then you'll do it?" Quick demanded.

Reo shrugged. His eyes had gone bleak. "You only
get one shot at life. Ain't no point in doing it stony
broke."

"That's what I always say," Quick agreed.

Antonia's eyes shone. She hip-swayed across the
room and pressed herself against Reo. She kissed his
mouth, grinned, and went back to Quick. Her knife
flashed; she began to saw at the ropes that bound his
hands.

"Hurry up," Quick complained.

Reo said, "I don't mind throwing down on Koenig.
Don't like him much anyhow. But I don't ordinarily
make war on women."

"You backing out?"

"I'm going to have to think on it," Reo said. He
turned to the window and took aim—and at that pre-
cise moment all three of them were shaken by an
ear-splitting explosion that rocked the walls of the
house.

Chapter Sixteen

THE blast knocked Buchanan flat against the
wall. He virtually had to peel himself off. He blinked
and got his balance, then hacked his way through the
billowing smoke. The groans and cries of men filled the
confinement of the room. The stink was suffocating.
Buchanan bowled into someone in the swirling fog—
Race Koenig.

"What the hell?" Buchanan said.

Koenig coughed. "They must've got their hands on that keg of blasting powder in the tack shed."

A six-foot halo of light streamed where the bolted front door had been. Buchanan saw shapes weave into sight—unmistakable by their shoulder-length hair, the flopped-over tops of their knee-length moccasins, the squat, broad shapes of their bodies.

The Apaches had blown down the front door. They were coming in.

Buchanan had lost his rifle somehow in the explosion. His hand whipped down, brought up the six-gun, and balanced it on the flat, wide shape of an Indian in the swirling light. He fired and saw the man go down.

Another silhouette took the place of the first. Koenig fired twice, and the silhouette staggered back. Shoulder to shoulder, Buchanan and Koenig stood in the center of the room and braced their withering fire against the weaving Indians who appeared, half vague, in the light.

Within seconds other cowhands joined in. A vicious volleying blasted through every square inch of the opening.

It drove the Apaches back, stumbling over the corpses of their comrades. Some stooped to drag fallen friends away with them. Buchanan reloaded feverishly and stalked toward the doorway. Beside him, Race Koenig was cursing in awe. "Jesus. Looks like the set of the last act of *Hamlet* out there."

Somebody said half hysterically, "It's all that readin' that done made Race nearsighted. I allus knowed that." A cackle of laughter drifted eerily through the smoke.

Buchanan flattened himself just inside the jagged edge of the blown-out door. He peered around cautiously.

What he saw stiffened all his joints.

Rumbling toward the doorway like a ghost wagon was a coach full of flames.

The Apaches were pushing the Pitchfork buckboard straight toward the open doorway. Piled high with hay and set afire, the buckboard was a wheeled dread-naught, spouting flames twenty feet into the sky.

Buchanan wheeled into the doorway and began to fire with grim, deadly fury. His bullets whizzed under and past the buckboard, chopping down legs, pinking arms, drilling through any half inch of flesh visible. Koenig rushed out and added the roar of his gun to the loud confusion. The searing heat of the flames burned hot against Buchanan's smoke-blackened face. Above the charred cheekbones, his hard eyes burned like jew-els. His gun blasted with deliberate, unhurried anger; and before the hail of bullets from Buchanan's and the others' guns, the Apaches who'd been pushing the wag-on broke and ducked away to find the nearest cover.

Buchanan's slug found one of them, pitched him rolling to the ground. Then his gun was empty.

Johnny Reo shifted into the doorway beside him, beside Koenig. Reo slip-hammered his six-gun, carving a wicked hole in the ranks of the running Apaches. Buchanan distinctly heard Reo's grim, low-pitched laughter.

The wagon, its momentum built up, kept coming. It rolled ponderously forward, straight for the doorway; above the rumble of its wheels crackled the roar of the fire, blue-hot and raging, whipped up by the wind.

"*Come on!*" Buchanan roared hoarsely. Ramming his gun into holster, he sprinted for the wagon and butted his shoulder against it, digging in his boots. The wagon almost capsized him; but then Koenig and Reo were with him, bending their weight against the buck-board. Flames licked around them. Somewhere Reo had lost his hat; his hair was indistinguishable in color from the flames. Buchanan felt his eyebrows singing. From the doorway half a dozen guns of the Pitchfork crew provided a heavy covering fire.

The wagon squeaked to a stop. Buchanan yanked the sleeves of his companions and made it back to the house on the run. A bullet scored the edge of his boot; an arrow thwacked into the adobe not six inches from his shoulder; and then, propelling Reo and Koenig ahead of him, he was pitching inside the smoky house. He fell over a crouching cowboy and slammed onto the floor.

Someone picked him up—Reo. Reo's grin was broad and white against his burned flesh.

"Jesus," someone said.

Buchanan wheeled. He saw the cowboy named Boat, laid out unnaturally on the floor just in the center of the doorway. An arrow had hit him in the face. Boat's right eyeball was hanging out on his cheek by a string of tissue.

Johnny Reo swallowed. "Christ, what an ugly way to die."

"Johnny, there are no pretty ways," said Buchanan. His eyes searched the stinging billows of smoke. He saw Marinda's blonde hair; she was unhurt. Koenig was with her. Cowhands stood just beside the jambs of the jagged doorway, keeping watch. There was a stretch of silence, uncanny and strange after the holocaust. Now and then a single shot boomed.

Buchanan loaded his gun and stepped to the door. He had a look outside. Down past the barn the Apaches were regrouping. He saw a sawed-off figure in a tall stovepipe hat, arms waving, voice lifting in husky rage, injecting bitter wrath into his speech with wild thrusts of his arms.

"We've got to stop this," Buchanan said. He took a rifle from a man beside him. "I'm sorry, old man," he muttered. He braced the rifle against the door jamb, calculated the elevation for extreme range, and killed Sentos with one clean-placed shot.

Buchanan's eyes were bleak and hollow. Haggard and morose, he stood in the dusty yard with the rifle dangling at arm's length. He was watching the disgusted remnants of the Apache war party scatter across the desert.

Race Koenig said, "It'll take them a while to pick

themselves a new chief. And by that time they'll be
cooled off enough not to come back."

Buchanan was glad the Apaches had taken Sentos'
body with them. He wouldn't have wanted to have to
bury the old warrior.

Cowhands limped across the yard, carrying their
wounded. Three or four men were dragging Apache
bodies out of the yard. Nobody went near the burning
buckboard, nobody had energy enough to try putting
out the fire. It would burn itself out.

In the house shutters slammed, coming open. It
would be days before the house could be aired out. To
build a new massive front door would take considerable
time.

Johnny Reo came outside rubbing his hip. "Judas
Priest. Empty shell cases like glass marbles all over the
floor in there. I about busted my butt."

Buchanan nodded, bounced the rifle in the circle of
his fist, and turned back into the house. Three men
were cleaning up the debris in the parlor. It looked as if
an earthquake had hit. Buchanan put the rifle down
and went back toward the kitchen, figuring to wash his
face and hands at the pump.

When he pushed the kitchen door open, he found
before his eyes a tableau that shocked him more than
anything he had seen in this battle-packed day.

Marinda was at the sink, wringing cloth bandages
under the pump. And behind her, moving stealthily,
Antonia was raising a long-bladed kitchen knife, ready
to plunge it into Marinda's unsuspecting back.

To distract Antonia, Buchanan slammed the door as
hard as he could, and in the same motion he leaped
forward.

Antonia jerked around with a start. Her mouth
sprang open; and then Buchanan was on her, wrenching her arm down, yanking the knife out of her grasp.

"You big son of a bitch," she snarled, "you've
spoiled everything you could, ever since you set foot on
this place."

"You don't look so pretty when you get mad," Buchanan told her. He tossed the knife aside.

Marinda was watching it all, not yet comprehending entirely. She said, "What . . . ?"

Antonia's heavy, sensuous lips curled back. She spat at Marinda. "You. I wish those Indians had raped you and burned you at the stake with no clothes on. If it hadn't been for you, this ranch would have been mine. It should have been."

Marinda frowned at her, puzzled. "What?"

Antonia's big breasts heaved with anger. She tossed her dark hair defiantly. Which was when two men came into the room—Steve Quick and Johnny Reo.

Antonia wheeled away from Buchanan and began to curse in low monotony. "Kill them," she said. "Kill both of them."

Quick's eyes widened. He snapped his glance toward Reo. "They're all that stands between us and Pitchfork, Reo."

Reo licked his lips. "You're crazy."

"I'll make it a half-interest in the place," Quick said in sudden desperation. "Half of the whole kit and kaboodle."

Buchanan's smoke-dusty face was working into a frown. "I wouldn't do it, Johnny. I wouldn't even think about doing it."

Marinda said angrily, "What's gotten into all of you? Steve, you've gone too far."

"I was born too far," Quick said tautly. "Go on, Reo."

Buchanan said quietly, "Forget it, Johnny. I've taken a liking to you. We've gone through a lot together—too much to let gold get in the way."

"Half of the whole works, Reo," Quick breathed. His pale eyes were wide with excitement and fear; he was backing up against the wall, his hand hanging near his gun.

Reo said, "Sorry, Buchanan. Money speaks louder than words." The familiar brash grin flashed across his cheeks.

Buchanan shook his head. "I won't draw first on you."

"You may as well. Because I'm going to draw on you."

"It'll be the biggest mistake you've ever made," Buchanan told him. "It'll be that whichever way it comes out."

"I recollect I told you never to count on me," Johnny Reo said. "Not where money's concerned. *Now pull steel, Buchanan!*"

And Johnny Reo flashed for his gun.

Buchanan's gun. It blazed, a single dazzling spear of muzzle flash and a single deafening roar of sound. The slug slammed through Reo's flesh and bone, ramming him back against the wall, throwing him across the arm of Steve Quick, who was desperately trying to claw his gun up. Quick thrust the obstruction away and shouted hysterically, yanking his gun up. Buchanan watched bleakly, and when Quick's thumb reached out to cock the gun, Buchanan fired twice.

The two big bullets pitched Steve Quick to the floor on rubber legs.

Buchanan's gun slipped back into its holster. Buchanan walked forward and knelt by Johnny Reo.

"How're you makin' it, amigo?"

Reo said numbly, "I started my draw first and I never got a shot fired."

"It was the biggest mistake, Johnny."

"Yeah." Reo coughed weakly. "Funny how your whole life can run out a tiny little hole like this. Like you pulled the plug on a drain. Know something, Buchanan? I think you've killed me."

"I'm sorry, amigo."

"I know you are." Reo smiled vaguely. "Anyhow, it don't hurt none. But hell, I always wanted to go out dead drunk with a bottle in my hand. Too bad about that. Buchanan?"

"Yes, Johnny?"

"I've been obliged to know you, amigo. I really have." Reo grinned then. His eyes rolled up lifelessly in their sockets.

Buchanan reached out and closed the lids.

Marinda stood just outside the gaping hole where the door had been. She watched Buchanan lead his horse forward and test the cinch. Race Koenig put his arm around Marinda and said, "I wish you'd stay on, Buchanan."

"Afraid I've got an appointment," Buchanan said. "Some fish to catch up in the mountains." He looked around the yard and added, "Besides, it's about time I gave some other place a potshot at me."

Marinda said very softly, "Thank you, Buchanan," and turned quickly to go inside.

Buchanan said, "Hey, lady."

"Yes?" She turned around.

He said, "I just wanted another look at you."

It made her smile, with tears close beneath; she said, "I'll cry at your wedding, Buchanan," and hurried into the house.

Two cowboys came out of the barn leading a saddle horse and prodding Antonia roughly in front of them. Koenig took off his eyeglasses, blew on the lenses, wiped them clean, and hooked them back on over his ears. He said to Antonia, "Keep going until you're clear out of the Territory. You show your face in Arizona again, and I'll have a bench warrant sent out for you."

"All right, Race," she said in a muted voice.

"And make sure none of the Pitchfork herd attaches itself to you on your way out."

She flashed. "I'm no cattle rustler."

"I wouldn't put anything past you."

Buchanan said mildly, "I'll see she gets on her way," and climbed onto his horse. Settling into the saddle, he

watched Antonia mount. His eyes studied her speculatively, the soft, ample curves of her body. He grinned
and nodded at her. "You ride in front of me," he said.

It promised to be an interesting ride.